WASHOE COUNTY
LIBRARY SYSTEM
www.washoecountylibrary.us

Items that you checked out

Title: Alien envoy /
ID: 31235035440531
Due: Saturday, March 14, 2020

Total items: 1
Account balance: $0.00
2/22/2020 1:52 PM
Checked out: 1
Overdue: 0
Hold requests: 0
Ready for pickup: 0

Thank you for using the Washoe County
Library System

alien envoy

aLiEn envoy

BOOK #6 OF THE
[aLiEn agent]
series

pameLa F.
service

illustrated by
mike gorman

darbycreek
MINNEAPOLIS

Darby Creek
A division of Lerner Publishing Group, Inc.
241 First Avenue North
Minneapolis, MN 55401 U.S.A.

Website address: www.lernerbooks.com

Library of Congress Cataloging-in-Publication Data

Service, Pamela F.
    Alien envoy / by Pamela F. Service ; illustrated by Mike Gorman.
      p.   cm. — (Alien agent ; #6)
    Summary: Agent Sorn picks Zack up from Earth and together they seek other aliens
who can speak in support of inviting that planet to join the Galactic Union, while the
Gnairt and the Kiapa Kapa Syndicate try to stop them.
    ISBN: 978-0-7613-5364-5 (trade hard cover : alk. paper)
    [1. Extraterrestrial beings—Fiction. 2. Interplanetary voyages—Fiction. 3. Science
fiction.] I. Gorman, Mike, ill. II. Title.
PZ7.S4885Alc 2011
[Fic]—dc22   2010009251

Manufactured in the United States of America
1 – SB –12/31/10

[alien agent] series

For Robert and Virginia

—P.S.

Prologue

Agent Sorn was in her apartment at the Galactic Union Headquarters, enjoying a rare day off. Curled up with her entertainment viewer, she sat reading what her boss would probably call a trashy novel. She was greatly enjoying it.

The door buzzer shrilled. Annoyed, she looked at the identifier to see who was waiting. Her boss. With a yelp, she switched off her novel and jumped to her feet. Chief Agent Zythis, with his multiple eyes and tentacles, stood outside.

She pressed a button and the door slid open. Zythis slithered in. "Agent Sorn, I apologize for intruding. But a crisis has arisen regarding one of the planets within your jurisdiction."

Sorn's heart sank. She was the prime Galactic Patrol agent for a rather remote sector of the galaxy. Several of those planets could be trouble, but danger threatened one more often than the others. She was afraid she knew what Zythis's next word would be. She was right.

"Earth," he sighed.

Sorn gestured to a large chair that would support Zythis's multi-tentacled shape. He settled in and continued. "You know that recent events have upped our timetable for inviting the planet to join the union."

She nodded impatiently. Of course she knew. She and the Alien Agent planted on Earth, Zack Gaither, had been part of those "recent events." But if it hadn't been for Zack, things could have been a great deal worse. "As I understand it," she said, "the Galactic Council is due to consider Earth's formal invitation shortly. Has that changed?"

"No, but through my spies I have learned that the Gnairt and the Kiapa Kapa Syndicate are trying to sabotage that effort. Our agent there may be endangered."

That grabbed Sorn's attention. Zack Gaither was developing into an excellent agent, but she still felt guilty that he had been thrust into Galactic Union matters before being fully trained. Zack hadn't even been aware that he was an alien living among humans until a couple of years ago.

Zythis cleared his several throats. "The Kiapa Kapa have caused enough trouble already by trying to take over Earth and its resources themselves. But now they are spreading rumors that the planet's not suited to becoming a Galactic Union member. What's more, it seems that our agent has been identified. There may be a plot to abduct or kill him to prevent him from serving as the union's envoy to planet Earth."

Sorn gasped. Zack's identity had been kept secret not only from most humans but from enemy aliens as well. "That's terrible! We must stop it."

Zythis's eye flaps wiggled as he nodded in agreement. "I have reread all of your earlier reports and have notified certain agents that they are needed to testify on behalf of Earth. You will take the fastest ship available, collect those agents from their current assignments, proceed to Earth for Agent Zack, and then return here to await the council hearing."

"Has Agent Zack been notified?"

"We dare not do so directly. There is reason to believe that the enemy has hacked into our communication system. Any notice will have to be carefully coded in such a way that you, as one familiar with Earth culture, believe he can understand and they cannot. You must contact him and then depart immediately."

After Chief Agent Zythis had left, Sorn cast a regretful last glance toward her unfinished novel. Then she plunged into her urgent assignment. The comforting thing about her novels was that she knew that whatever adventures and dangers took place, things would work out in the end. Any dealings she'd had with Earth involved more than enough adventure and danger, but they were real. They never came with the promise of a happy ending.

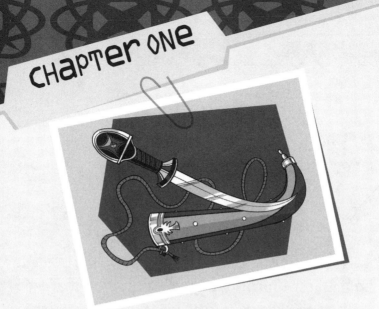

CHAPTER ONE

Halloween. My favorite holiday. I've always loved the crisp fall air, with its scents of burning leaves and excitement. Dressing as something that you aren't, staying out after hours, roaming the dark streets with other mysterious figures, and collecting usually forbidden treats—all part of a great night for any human kid.

Even now that I'd learned I wasn't human, and after I'd had more excitement than most, I still loved Halloween. And this year, I wanted to savor every moment of it. Too many other things seemed to be changing in my life.

Our parents felt that my friend Ken and I were getting a little too old for trick-or-treating.

We didn't agree. But we compromised and said we'd go to the Halloween dance party at the school instead—and quietly do some trick-or-treating on the way to and from.

This Halloween fell on a Saturday, so I had all day to put together my costume. And to worry about the odd message I'd just received from Agent Sorn on my computer. It made so little sense it was like it was in code or something: "Be a motto Boy Scout. Do what you need with your old kit bag, and smile, smile, smile. Beware little pitchers."

What the heck could that mean?

I knew that on one of her last trips to Earth, Sorn had picked up a book about Earth slang and old sayings. In her communications, she sometimes asked me about their meaning. Often they were way out of date. Was this just some fun puzzle? Or, if it was in code, was it something important?

The first part I got quickly. "Be a motto Boy Scout." At first I thought it was supposed to say "a model Boy Scout," but then I guessed it did mean "motto." I'm not a scout, but I have friends who are. Their motto is "Be Prepared." That chilled me a little. Prepared for what?

The rest was gibberish to me, so I took it to my parents. I'm really glad now that my parents have finally learned that I'm not a human child like they'd thought they'd adopted. And I'm even gladder that they don't care. They still consider me their son. And they're even sort of okay with the Alien Agent thing, though I know they worry about me.

It was my dad who cracked the next part. After puzzling a bit, he suddenly smiled and broke into a really lame little song. "Pack up your troubles in your old kit bag, and smile, smile, smile." He said it was an old World War I song. My dad is not *that* old, but he's a teacher and knows about that kind of stuff.

He couldn't figure out the last bit, but Mom finally did. "Little pitchers have big ears!" she suddenly exclaimed. "My grandmother used to say that when she caught us kids listening in on things we weren't supposed to."

The "little pitchers" thing was scary. Sorn must be afraid that someone, someone unfriendly, was reading our messages.

So I had the message. I was supposed to be prepared—for *something*. And I was supposed to pack. Though since I didn't know what or where that something was, packing was tough. I finally just stuffed a backpack with a change of clothes, toothbrush, flashlight, jackknife, compass, and binoculars. And, at my mom's insistence, the usual supply of granola bars.

Figuring I was as prepared as I could expect to be, I left the backpack by my bedroom door and concentrated on planning for Halloween. Ken was going as a two-headed space alien. I'd seen some weird-looking space aliens, but none with two heads. Still, I couldn't tell Ken that. I wasn't supposed to tell any humans what I was, though a few had sort of found out during some past assignments. So an alien costume was definitely not for me. After much thought, I decided on a pirate outfit.

In the end, I looked pretty dashing. Black jeans, my mom's black riding boots, a billowy white shirt, a purple bandanna, a beach-towel cape, one very uncomfortable clip-on earring, and a red sash. Stuck under the sash was the best part of all: a real curved dagger. Some exchange teacher from Morocco gave it to my dad. Well, it was actually a large letter opener, but it looked the part.

When Ken showed up at our door, his costume looked pretty cool too. The green tights and tunic had once been a Robin Hood costume. The spangled green cape was cut from his sister's old prom dress, and he wore green face makeup—on his own face. His other head was an already-green alien Halloween mask. It bobbed about on some springs attached to Ken's shoulder. His weapon was an impressive plastic ray gun. I'd seen real ones that didn't look nearly as convincing.

Some of the littlest trick-or-treaters had already hit our door, but now it was getting dark, and Mom had me light the smirking jack-o'-lantern before we set off. I took a second to whiff the hot wax and scorched pumpkin. Then Halloween called.

Slipping trick-or-treat bags under our capes, we set out to ring doorbells. My favorite loot is candy corn or peanut butter cups. Got plenty of those. One place had buckets of lollipops, which I've never much liked. And the guy who gave out candied prunes ought to be jailed.

Munching on candy as we headed toward the school, Ken grumbled, "I don't know why my parents think I'm too old for trick-or-treating. Lots of older kids are out. Even adults are in costume today. Like those fat, bald guys back there. What are they dressed as? Tweedledee and Tweedledum?"

That zapped through my Halloween fun like a laser. Two fat, bald guys? I spun around. Further back along the sidewalk, the streetlight showed two figures who could have been those *Alice's Adventures in Wonderland* twins. Or they could have been a couple of Gnairt.

Stupid, I told myself. The world is full of fat, bald guys. These are probably a couple of skinny, hairy kids in costumes anyway. Still, I upped my pace. "Let's get to school and do the party thing," I said hurriedly. "We can leave early and add to our loot."

When we got there, the school gym was decorated with orange and black streamers and the usual Halloween cardboard cutouts: black cats, witches, pumpkins, and such. The planning committee had divided the gym floor into areas for apple bobbing, pin the tail on the unicorn (some of the girls on the committee had insisted), and a haunted house. The place was noisy with kids and music.

I kind of wanted to try the spook house but thought it might be lame. Ken and I decided to just stand outside and look smug until someone we trusted came out and said it was cool. We watched the dancing at one end of the gym. Finally, Ken said, "Want to dance?"

"With you?" I squeaked.

"No way! No, I mean there's a bunch of girls standing over there. This is supposed to be a dance—maybe we ought to ask someone."

He sputtered into silence. I prodded him a little. "You really want to?"

He grinned. "No. Forget it. I really can't think of any girl I'd like to dance with."

I couldn't either. Well, I had met a girl this last summer who might be kind of a fun dancing partner. But she lived miles and miles away and was probably at another Halloween party with her own friends.

Getting more and more bored, I scanned the crowd and suddenly froze. Impossible! I was supposed to have alien powers, not a genie's. But there was the very girl I'd just thought about: Shasta O'Neil. And yet the closer she walked toward me—straight toward me—the more it looked like her. Black braids, bronze skin, a troublemaking glint in her eye.

"Zack! I hardly recognized you in your dashing pirate outfit." She grabbed my hand. "But thank the spirits we found you!"

I stared at her a moment, turning as red as a fire engine. Then her words clicked. "We?" I managed to say. "Who else is . . . ?"

My eyes moved across the room and picked out the white hair and purple skin of Agent Sorn as she pushed her way through the crowd. Catlike Agent Khh was perched on her shoulder, his leathery wings tucked into his long fur.

"What . . . ? Why . . . ?"

By then Sorn had reached me.

"Agent Zack. We must leave immediately. You're in danger."

Suddenly she caught sight of Ken leaning on the other side of the pillar. "A Stritorian? I wouldn't have expected . . . Oh, I see. It's a costume. Sorry, the two heads fooled me." Then she turned back to me. "We went to your house, and your mother told us you'd be here. We brought your bag. Now you must leave."

Helplessly, I looked at Ken. Even under his green makeup he looked kind of stunned. "Ken, I'm sorry. I can't really explain now. But I've got to go with these people." I thrust my trick-or-treat bag at him and muttered, a little jealously, "Enjoy."

Our odd little group wormed its way through the crowd toward a side door. We hadn't taken many steps beyond the gym when claws grabbed my shoulders and pushed me to the asphalt. A blast of light smashed into the wall behind me.

A lot of teeth were suddenly in front of my face. "Stay down, idiot!"

"Vraj! What . . . ?"

"Crawl behind that metal thing," the dinosaur-like cadet agent hissed. "It's *you* they're after!"

Energy beams crisscrossed the parking lot as I scuttled behind the dumpster. I turned my head to see Ken step through the doorway. "Zack, what's . . . ?"

Leaping like a panther, I tackled Ken and dragged him with me behind the metal dumpster. Some kids on the far side of the lot were cheering like this was a light show, but I knew it was deadly. And I felt helpless just hiding there. I looked at Ken, his eyes huge and questioning.

"Let me borrow your ray gun."

"It's just a toy," he said, handing it to me.

"Right, but it's got a battery. I need some energy to work with."

I focused my mind on the silver tube, weaving the battery's energy with my own. Peering around the corner of the dumpster, I caught sight of a Tweedledee-shaped figure crouched behind a parked car. I aimed the toy gun. Energy blasted from its plastic barrel in a neon stream. The car erupted in a rush of orange flame.

"Oops," I groaned. "Overdid it."

"Wow!" Ken breathed beside me. "I don't know what's going on, but that was way cool." His eyes widened even farther as he caught sight of the sharp-toothed alien to the other side of me. "That's a costume your friend's wearing," Ken said, his voice almost pleading. "A velociraptor outfit. Right?"

I looked nervously back at him. "Ken, this is complicated, but very important. I'll explain later. I promise. But for now, please tell people you didn't see anything and don't know anything. Okay?"

Both his heads nodded, but only his real one beamed. "Hey, you think I'm nuts? If I try to talk about this, I'll be locked up. Look, Zack, I don't know what on Earth . . . or wherever . . . is going on. But I won't tell on you. Good luck!"

Scuttling out from behind the dumpster, Vraj hauled me around the corner where the others had disappeared. Sorn, Shasta, and Khh weren't far away. They saw us and sprinted for the line of trees behind the gym. We followed.

I wasn't surprised to see a spaceship hidden there. It was shiny like a silver hubcap and shaped like a Hollywood flying saucer. Just as Sorn opened a hatch, another energy beam cut through the trees behind us, splintering branches across the lot. The beam sparked harmlessly over the surface of the ship.

"In!" Sorn ordered as she pulled out her own weapon and fired back. I didn't see if she hit anything. I was too busy charging up the ramp with the others.

Sorn dove in after us, closed the hatch, and settled behind a bank of controls. In seconds our ship quivered to life and rose from behind the screen of trees.

Looking through a port in the ship's curved side, I saw my school dropping away below us. A scattering of people were pointing upward. I even made out Ken, still beside the dumpster. He was waving.

A mixture of homesickness and excitement overwhelmed me. "Happy Halloween," I whispered.

CHAPTER TWO

It was hard to tear myself away from the view, but so many questions were fizzing up inside of me that I felt ready to explode. I looked toward the control area in the center of the ship. Sorn seemed to be busy flying the thing, and Vraj was seated at another console, studying a screen and jabbing buttons. Khh was curled up asleep on a chair, a wing wrapped around him like a blanket. The ship was at least much roomier than the others I'd ridden in. Shasta was smiling beside me.

"Can you tell me what's going on?" I asked her.

"I don't know a whole lot more than you. But right now I want to enjoy the view. Look, that's amazing!"

And it was. My hometown was just a sparkle of lights now. As we rose higher we could see other light clusters scattered through the darkness. "Do you know where we're going?" I whispered.

She squeezed my hand excitedly. "Space! We're actually going to the stars!"

Shasta's grandfather was this Native American medicine-person guy who'd told her that her future was tied up with star spirits. Sounds hokey, but I'd already seen too many strange things to make light of it. And anyway, I was pretty excited too. Sure, I'd been born on another planet, and maybe I'd actually get a chance to learn about it someday. But Earth had been my home as long as I could remember. I could share Shasta's excitement over the age-old human dream of going to other worlds.

I felt a hand on my shoulder. Sorn stood behind us, watching Earth slowly drop away.

"That's what all this is about," she said. "Earth. And its future."

She launched into a quick explanation of that weird coded message and why they'd snatched me away from the Halloween party. By the time she'd finished, I was majorly overwhelmed. It sounded like I was being asked to go speak for Earth in front of the United Nations of planets. Me, who gets a little queasy just getting up to speak in front of class. A class of humans, ones I'd grown up with.

Sorn must have read the terror in my face. She smiled. "You won't be alone. The rest of us are here because we've had some contact with Earth and can speak for it. Also, we've downloaded lots of information from your planet's Internet. Earth's history, culture, and so forth. The delegates will learn how much Earth can contribute to the Galactic Union."

I wasn't sure how great an idea that was, considering some of Earth's history. Apparently Shasta had the same thought. "You know there's some kind of dark stuff in our history."

Sorn nodded. "All species go through 'dark stuff.' If they don't destroy themselves, most grow out of it."

I looked at Shasta. I was glad she was there, but still a little confused. "So . . . uh . . . how come . . . "

"I'm here?" She laughed. "Sorn e-mailed me. Cool, since I'd never gotten an e-mail from another planet before! She told me what was happening and asked if I was willing to come along. As if I'd miss a chance like this! She even fitted me with one of those translator bugs, like you have."

I frowned. "You didn't tell . . . "

"Hey, I can play secret agent too. I told my family I was doing National Parks stuff and the parks people that I was doing family stuff. Not that anybody would have believed the truth if I'd tried it on them."

"I thought it would be best to have an actual human along to speak for Earth as well," Sorn added. "And Shasta has shown herself to be resourceful and talented before. There was no way the opposition would be bugging her computer, so I could explain things in detail. But now I'll get back to the controls. We don't like to jump into transluminal space until we're on the far side of the asteroid belt, where Earth astronomers can't accidentally see the flash."

At that moment, an alarm shrilled through the ship. We all rushed toward the console, where Vraj was jabbing buttons with her sharp claws. A magnified image appeared on a viewscreen. From out of a swarm of floating rocks, a ship zoomed toward us.

"Incoming unidentified ship," Vraj announced, her claws eagerly hovering over some other buttons. Khh had awoken and was perched on her shoulder.

"Should I fire?" Vraj asked, teeth glinting hungrily.

"Wait. That looks like a Nythian ship," Sorn said as she fiddled with more controls. After a moment, the image on our viewscreen shifted from the approaching ship's teardrop-shaped outside to its interior. The occupants looked very familiar.

"It's Iv and Tu!" I cried. "The aliens I met in Roswell."

The taller of the small grey humanoids raised a four-fingered hand in greeting. "Well met, Zack. And Galactic Union Agent Sorn, I presume. We heard that you were searching for witnesses to testify on behalf of Earth. Since I spent over sixty years on the planet, I thought I could help, particularly after all the help Zack gave me and Tu."

The shorter alien looked directly at me with his large, slanted, black eyes. "And I won't let my dad go anywhere without me. Not after all the trouble he got into last time."

Iv laughed with his son, then sobered. "But right now we've got to warn you. A bunch of ships are waiting just beyond the asteroid belt. I suspect it's an ambush."

"Kiapa Kapa," Sorn muttered. Then she addressed the screen. "Thanks for the warning. Bring your ship into our loading dock and come on board. We have some evading to do."

In minutes, the two little grey aliens were among

us. Shasta was really impressed. "Now that's what I expected aliens to look like. Just like in movies."

"Makes sense," I said. "It was Iv who gave the moviemakers that idea after he crashed on Earth years ago."

Most of the others started arguing about the best way to evade the enemy and get to Galactic Union Headquarters. I hadn't a clue about any of that, but the viewscreen picture was suddenly troubling. "Hey, are those dots moving among the asteroids more ships?"

Argument turned into a flurry of action, with Shasta and me trying to stay out of the way.

"Defensive shields up!"

"Ready the weapons!"

"Plot an evasive escape route!"

"Look out!"

(That last one was me, after a volley of lights suddenly zapped toward us on the screen.)

Our ship bucked and then zipped off in a new direction. Explosions of light blossomed everywhere. I lay sprawled on the floor as we spiraled away.

"Jump to transluminal space!" Sorn shouted.

"What coordinates?" Vraj yelled over an ominous new hum from the ship's engines.

"Random ones," Sorn answered. "That'll make it harder for them to follow."

A new volley of lights burst around us. Suddenly they were gone. Everything was. No explosions, no stars. Only colorful streaks of light smeared against blackness. I felt all hollow and squashed, like I was rising in a very fast elevator.

Sitting beside me on the floor, Shasta looked as weirded-out as I felt. "What's going on?"

"I think we've just switched to a faster-than-light kind of travel. I don't know how it works exactly, but that's how these space people can move across the galaxy without it taking thousands of years."

"Cool. But it sure feels odd."

What felt oddest was that my internal clock seemed to have turned off. I had no sense of how much time was passing, seconds or years. One thing I *did* have a sense of, though, was sound. The alarming engine hum got louder, filling the ship. What was really alarming about it was how much it alarmed the others.

"How much damage did we sustain?" Sorn asked as Iv and Vraj studied various screens.

"Too much," Vraj growled. "We'll never get to headquarters without repairs."

Sorn frowned. "Can we do them here in transluminal space?"

"No way, José," Khh said from his perch on Iv's shoulder. He enjoyed using Earth terms, even out-of-date ones. "Repairs have got to be done in real time."

"All right. Scan for any planets we're passing that have breathable atmospheres. Choose one at random to reduce chances of the enemy figuring out where we've gone."

Tu watched the others plot a course for a while. Then he walked over kind of shyly and showed me and Shasta his collection of holographic trading cards. In Earth years, he'd be a century old, and he'd been going to school so long that he knew a huge amount about space technology. But he was still a kid as far as his species was concerned.

Those cards of his were cool. They showed various alien species on their native planets. The pictures were 3-D and moved. Tu's aim was to collect one for every species in the Galactic Union. He said he still had a ways to go. That didn't help my nerves any. I was supposed to speak to an audience full of hundreds of folks like that. There were some awfully unnerving aliens in his collection, like the one who was all mouth or the one who looked like a flying dog dropping.

Anyway, looking at the cards helped pass the time. And I suppose time was passing, though I didn't feel tired or hungry or anything. Then suddenly the ship quivered, the stars reappeared, and I felt like I'd just smashed against the top of the elevator shaft.

"This'll do," Vraj said. "The surface is a little unstable, but solid enough to land on."

We watched through the viewport as a planet drew closer. Shasta and I grinned at each other. A real alien planet! It certainly didn't look much like Earth. Stretches of purple that might be oceans or plains were broken up by blue-grey stuff we thought might be mountains. Some of these spots were fringed in lacy white.

"Any inhabitants?" Sorn asked.

Iv consulted a screen. "Animal life, some plant life. No civilization."

"Take us down."

The ship was making more whining, grating sounds as we neared the planet. We seemed to be heading toward the smooth, purple surface. I really hoped we landed before the ship fell apart.

The purple ground was coming fast. With a quiver and a thrum, we landed.

"Now we'll run tests and see what can be done to fix this tub," Sorn said. Then she turned to Shasta, Tu, and me. "The sensors show nothing hostile out there. You three go out and romp. Just stay near the ship."

I should have been offended. Treated like a little kid let out on a wiggle break during a long car ride! But really there wasn't a thing Shasta or I could've done to help fix the ship. Tu probably could have helped—he was awfully good at mechanical things—but his dad was good at them too. And this was my first alien planet! The first I had any recollection of anyway.

The hatch opened, the ramp slid down, and we three eagerly trotted out. At the bottom of the ramp I leapt onto the planet's solid-looking surface. I'd expected to land on something like desert. It felt more like a vast sheet of grape Jell-O.

CHAPTER THREE

The ground was slick and rubbery. Shasta, Tu, and I bounded across it in huge jumps like it was a gigantic trampoline. The gravity there must be a lot less intense than Earth's, because I felt like a movie ninja, twisting in the air and making impossibly long leaps.

I have to admit, we did sound like three little kids let out to play, squealing and laughing. After some experimenting, we figured out how to control our leaps and do fancy gymnastics in the air. We kept bouncing farther and farther away from the ship, but since we could control the direction of our jumps it didn't bother us.

Sometime during the fun I noticed that the surface seemed to be trembling from more than just our jumping. A sudden lurch sent us skidding wildly over the smooth purple sheet. The surface underneath us abruptly dropped down into a trough. We rolled to the bottom. Just as abruptly, the ground rose up into a hill, taking us up with it. Land that had seemed solid, if bouncy, now rolled along under us like a giant purple tidal wave. Lying flat on our stomachs, we were surfing along its crest.

Not as fun as it sounds. Downright scary, in fact.

The rubbery wave took us ever closer to what had been a distant ridge. The blue-grey rock looked very hard. For all we knew, the lacy white stuff at its base was sharp crystal, or maybe thorny plants. And it was all coming closer.

And closer. The rock towered over us now. With a final heave, the purple wave flung us forward. I fell through the air and was engulfed in white. Plants surrounded me. Not thorny ones. More like dry and brittle. They crackled as I plunged through them, releasing a smell like strong garlic.

I lay still at the bottom of a hedge, looking at the distant green sky through a web of broken white twigs. I heard plants snapping where Shasta and Tu must have fallen. Then there was another noise, a sharp beeping like a smoke detector running out of batteries. It came from underneath me.

I looked down. Partly beneath me lay a pale, purple, feathery thing. It was flat and round, about the size of a pie plate, and had three eyestalks rising from the center. Alien or not, the look in those eyes was reproachful. A couple of short, stumpy legs splayed out from the creature's rim, but several more legs seemed to be wriggling underneath me.

"Oh, sorry little fellow," I said, rolling over enough to free it. The animal kept beeping and flopped feebly. It looked like I'd bent or broken some of its legs.

I felt bad. The little thing hadn't asked for me to come crashing down on it. I carefully picked it up. Three legs flopped down uselessly. Sorn was really good at healing, and she'd been trying to teach me. She'd said my species could manipulate cell molecules as well as energy, but I hadn't managed much so far. Better try anyway, I thought.

I concentrated, probing with my mind. The little creature's anatomy was very simple, so it was clear where the damage was. I held the three limp legs with one hand and mentally tried to straighten them. The creature's beeping slowly softened into a purr. Suddenly it flapped out of my hands and kind of floated upward.

I suddenly saw that a bunch of its fellow fluffy creatures had gathered to watch. All of them, my patient included, fluttered upward through the crater I'd made in the plants. They sounded like small, purring helicopters.

I didn't watch them long. A crashing sound from my left was followed by Shasta's voice. "Anyone hurt?"

"I'm okay," I answered. "Low gravity's good for falling, I guess."

More crashing from my right. "These plants smell bad," Tu said as he pushed his way through the brittle brush.

"No, I like it," Shasta said as she joined us. "Kind of strong, though. Like an explosion in a pizza factory."

I smiled, happy to see my companions unhurt. "You'd think that with all that purple, this planet would smell like grape."

"We better get out of this white stuff," Tu said as he patted a device on his belt. "I tried to signal our general location. My father could take our little ship and come scouting for us. But he'd never find us down here."

We decided that if we walked in a straight line, we'd come to the edge of the plants eventually. They'd only formed a narrow band between the purple plains and the blue-grey rocks. I decided the rocks were what we wanted to head for—we could climb up and get a better idea of where the ship was.

Now that we weren't falling, the plants were hard to just push aside. But then I remembered the cool Moroccan dagger in my pirate costume belt. Using it like a machete, I went first, hacking our way through the brush. It was easy to keep going straight because we could look back and see our path carved through the brittle plants. I felt bad about the damage until I noticed that, far behind us, the ragged tunnel already seemed to be closing up.

Finally we broke out of the white hedge and found ourselves looking up at a steep, rocky slope. The rock itself was grey. Splotches of blue moss swept over it.

"Let's climb a ways so we can see over the plants," I suggested. "I hope the ship wasn't hurt in the Jell-O-quake or whatever. I guess when the sensors said there were no hostile life forms out here, they weren't thinking about the planet itself."

Shasta gave me a sharp look, then began to climb. "This planet is not hostile."

Tu and I followed. "The plants aren't, at least," Tu observed. "The stinky white bushes and the blue moss aren't trying to eat us.

My father once landed on a planet where the grass crawled up his legs and tried to strangle him."

"I saw some animals," I added. "Flat with lots of legs, fluffy and purple."

Shasta quickly corrected me: "Lavender. I saw them too."

"Whatever. Anyway, they didn't attack me, even though I'd accidentally hurt one. Still, I guess it's not fair to blame the purple tsunami for throwing us here. Whatever that stuff is, it's just the planet's surface. It's not alive."

Suddenly Shasta plunked herself down on a boulder and glared at me. "Honestly, don't you feel it? This planet is very alive."

"You can sense life?" Tu asked, obviously impressed.

She looked down like she was embarrassed. "Well, not like that really." Then she looked up at me. "Zack, remember how I told you that my grandfather was a medicine man? Well, he didn't just have visions of the future. He could communicate with spirits. Rock spirits, tree spirits, spirits of the land. He said I had an even stronger power. He was trying to teach me so I could take his place. I was sort of catching on, but I wasn't really all that interested. There was school, my volunteer parks job, hanging out with my friends. But here . . . well, it's hitting me like a hammer."

"There are spirits here?" Tu said, looking around nervously.

Shasta nodded in a dreamy way. "I'm wondering if maybe all worlds have spirits. My people's stories always say that spirits were the first people. But as we humans got busier and made machines, we stopped listening to them. Or they stopped having much to say to us. This world doesn't have a bunch of cities and cars and cell towers and such. Maybe its spirits are easier to detect."

What she said made sense—in a weird sort of way. I'd wondered about this a bit before. Here I had all these nonhuman alien powers that I was just learning to use. But maybe humans had some sort of psychic or whatever powers that I didn't have. Maybe some had ways of talking with their world, ways that civilization kind of covered up. Every country on Earth had stories about "magic," after all.

It was all too heavy for me then. What we needed to do, I thought, was find a way to get back to our ship.

Tu was standing on a boulder and looking over the lacy white branches to the purple plain beyond. "I think I see it."

Shasta and I quickly joined him, but neither of us could make out anything. We knew, though, that Tu's big, dark eyes were a lot better than ours.

"It looks like the ship flipped upside down," he said. "We have to make sure no one's hurt!"

The fact that no one had come looking for us wasn't a good sign. I hoped it just meant that Tu and Iv's little ship was now damaged too, or that they couldn't get the hold's hatch open. "We'd better make our way back to the purple plain, fast."

"Bad idea," Shasta said, pointing to the horizon.

This planet's sun was a bright blue-white. And suddenly I realized it was very close to setting. The air, which had felt mild and pleasant up 'til now, was definitely taking on a chill.

I grunted. "Right. We'd better find some shelter and set out in the morning."

"Unless this planet's nights are really long," Tu said.

That was an even more chilling thought. But Shasta shook her head. "They probably aren't. See, the sun's moving quickly. It looks even closer to the horizon already. But we'd better look for a cave or something before the light goes."

We began scrambling over the tumbled rocks. Lots of crevasses, but no place big enough to give the three of us much shelter. The sun slid beyond the horizon, for a moment making the whole plain glow a jewel-like purple.

Twilight smothered us in a grey blanket, blurring all the rocks around us into a feature-less mass. The air was soon much colder. I was glad I was still wearing my beach-towel cape.

"Over here!" Tu cried out of the dimness farther up the slope. "I was watching a little lizard thing and it scuttled into a big cave."

Not very big, I saw when we got there, but big enough for the three of us. The rock walls around the cave entrance cut off the wind nicely. We settled down on a flat ledge in front of the cave. Tu took out a tool from his belt and made a little bonfire from slabs of blue moss we pulled off the rocks. We huddled around the fire, wishing we had some food with us and watching stars in unfamiliar patterns appear in the alien sky.

After a long while, my eyes dropped from the sky, and I began looking at the rocks around us. The rocks and the shadows. The moving shadows.

Chills rippled through me. "Shasta," I whispered tensely, "I think maybe some of those spirits you mentioned are checking us out."

CHAPTER FOUR

Tu's eyes seemed even bigger than usual as he looked nervously into the encroaching dark. Shasta's eyes were closed. She was leaning back against the rock wall of the cave, but didn't look asleep. She seemed to be listening to something.

The shadows I had noticed slowly moved in. Our fire sank to glowing embers, and the shadows began swirling around the cave like smoke. I stared at them, but no sooner did I half make out a shape than it would shift to something else. There were sounds too. Voices.

My language implant was supposed to let me understand most alien languages, but the meaning of the words I heard now faded in and out. It wasn't me they were talking to, anyway. It was Shasta. She spoke back to them in a language I couldn't catch and a voice almost too soft to hear.

Hours seemed to pass. Then, in a swirl of darkness, the shadows blew away and into the night. Our fire flared up again, and Shasta opened her eyes.

"I wish my grandfather could have been here," she sighed. "They had so much to say."

"Those were spirits?" Tu asked in an awed voice.

"Those were this world's first people, the spirits of this place. They have all the power here and fear that if others come their world will be taken from them."

I frowned. "Did you tell them we don't really want to be here and will leave as soon as our ship's fixed?"

"They know we mean no harm and have behaved well. No, what they fear are the beings they sense coming after us."

"The Kiapa Kapa!" Tu squeaked. "They must have tracked us."

Shasta nodded. "So we need to leave as soon as possible."

"But we're miles from our ship," I protested, "and it's damaged."

"Maybe we'll be helped. Anyway, it'll be dawn soon."

I looked beyond our ledge. The stars seemed fewer and fainter. We watched the sky slowly fade from black to grey and then to a soft green. Low in that sky, a new light appeared. It was moving our way.

Excitedly, Tu fiddled with the instruments on his belt. "My father!" he cried. "My father's coming. I'm signaling where we are."

Then there were more not-stars in the sky. Lots of them, high up.

"Looks like the bad guys have arrived!" Shasta said. "Tu, I sure hope your dad gets here soon."

He did. The teardrop-shaped ship skimmed over the band of white plants and soon hovered just beyond the ledge of our cave. As we scrambled across the ramp into the ship, we saw that the enemy ships were clustered over one distant spot on the purple plain.

Iv hugged his son, gestured for all of us to sit, then aimed his ship back the way he'd come. "It's been amazing," he said. "When that quake happened, Sorn's ship was flipped over and I couldn't get our little ship out. But a little while ago, the ground sort of burped. The big ship flipped over again, and I was able to get away."

"But now the Kiapa Kapa are attacking the others!" Tu wailed.

His father grimaced. "The others may be in trouble, but not just from the Syndicate." His voice was taut. "As soon as I took off and the Kiapa Kapa ships appeared, the ground opened up. It swallowed Sorn's ship whole."

"What about Sorn and Vraj and Khh?" I asked, flooded with worry.

"We'd just finished fixing the big ship— they were all inside when it was sucked down.

I only hope that gives them some protection now." He gestured out the front viewscreen. "Look!"

Beams of weapons fire shot down from the clustered enemy ships. They hit one patch of purple ground, and the beams bounced back! As we watched, the rebounding energy collided with an enemy ship. The craft burst into flaming shreds.

"What do we do now?" Tu asked, looking over his father's shoulder.

"Don't know," Iv replied. "I don't see any way we can help."

In fact, it was getting harder to see anything. The sky that had been clear at dawn was rapidly clouding over. Dark, bruise-colored clouds spilled over the horizon, cutting off the sun and spreading over the plain. The first of them, towering like a mountain, had nearly reached the enemy ships.

"What now?" Iv muttered to himself as he slowed his ship to a stop.

For the first time since the cave, Shasta spoke

up. "When the storm gets here, go low beneath the clouds. Head to where the ship's hidden."

Iv looked at her doubtfully, but I nodded. "Better listen to her. She's been talking with some of the locals."

Tu lowered his ship until it hovered just above the rubbery surface. When the roiling cloud cover reached us, we sped forward. Needles of lightning shot through the clouds above. Suddenly, below us, a huge purple bubble rose out of the ground. It quivered and then burst, spewing Sorn's ship into the air. The ship hovered there under its own power.

"Yes!" Shasta exclaimed. I wondered if she'd known this was going to happen.

In moments, Iv had docked our little ship in the bigger one's bay. When we made our way up to the control room, Sorn, Vraj, and Khh greeted us, then turned to pilot the ship through the narrow layer between storm and ground. Occasional blasts of energy sliced down through the sky, but we dodged them and swept on.

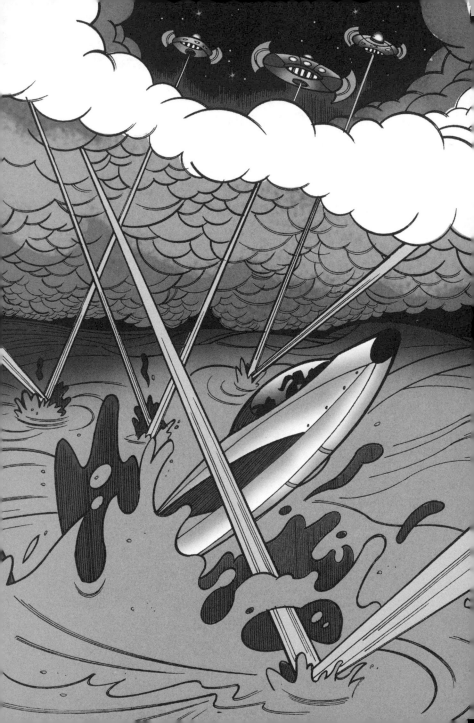

At the edge of the cloud covering, we shot up into clear green air. Several Syndicate ships gave chase behind us, firing as they came.

"Time for weapons now?" Vraj asked with a toothy grin.

"Absolutely," Sorn answered, and instantly Vraj was jabbing at a new set of controls. Our ship bucked slightly with each weapon's volley. Shasta and I looked out the rear screen, but it was hard to tell if Vraj made any hits because we couldn't see the enemy. The lightning-filled clouds had suddenly flung upward like a tossed blanket, smothering even the light of the energy weapons, ours and theirs.

"About to jump to transluminal space!" Sorn called. I barely had time to sit down before that wave washed over me, making me feel squashed and stretched at the same time. Outside the viewscreens, the planet had disappeared, and the stars were only colorful streaks against pulsing black.

Shasta was sitting cross-legged beside me on the floor, a thin smile on her face.

"So how did you like your first visit to an alien planet?" I asked, then blushed. That sounded kind of pompous, since it was basically my first alien planet too. But she didn't seem to mind.

"Amazing. I could never have imagined anything like that. The feel of the place, its spirits . . . well, that was amazing. I wonder, though, if maybe it wasn't really all that alien."

Kind of a deep thought. Could all planets have these "earth spirits" before other forms of life take over? This universe was turning out to be very weird. Very cool, too. And there I was, getting a chance to see it! Very, very cool—if I lived to remember anything I'd discovered.

Chapter Five

As transluminal space flowed past the viewscreens, I finally got my head and stomach together. Enough, anyway, to get off the floor and sit in one of the seats around the control center. Sorn and Vraj were still hunched over monitors, and Tu seemed to be studying star charts. Khh, perched on the back of Sorn's chair, looked like one of those crabby cathedral gargoyles.

"So now where are we heading?" the winged cat snapped. "That 'head to random coordinates' maneuver didn't work so well."

Vraj turned and glared at him. "Quiet! I think better when I'm not hungry. And I *am* hungry now," she said, her dagger-sharp teeth inches from Khh's whiskered face. Khh fluttered hastily back to a vacant seat and grumbled to himself.

"No eating fellow agents," Sorn said absently. "Still, that *is* the problem. Somehow the Syndicate ships managed to track us through transluminal space. We're safe from attack as long as we're in it, but they know we have to get to Galactic Union Headquarters. If we head there directly, they could have an ambush waiting for us. But if we try more evasion, it seems they can track us wherever we go."

"Isn't there anyplace safe we could head to?" Tu asked. He was sitting beside his dad now. For a moment I felt a pang, remembering how comforting it had always felt just being around my human father.

Iv frowned. "Well, we could go to our own planet, Nythia, but our weapons are no match for the Syndicate's."

Sorn nodded. "And we don't want to spark off an interstellar war. But I've another idea, a planet that might give us protection."

Everyone looked at her expectantly.

"Izbor," she said.

Khh spat. "They'd never even let us land. A planet of snooty recluses."

"Never heard of them," Vraj snarled.

"Generally," Sorn said, "they don't want to be heard of. Izborians are an ancient species. Eons ago they were very involved in galactic politics, but they have withdrawn from all that now. Even so, they are also a compassionate people and occasionally agree to help in some worthy cause."

Khh grumbled. "Sure, but is our little ship, or even Earth's admittance to the union, worthy enough for them?"

Sorn left her seat and, oddly enough, walked directly over to me. "In this case, perhaps. After all, Izbor is already slightly involved." Sorn put a hand on my shoulder.

I could see understanding flicker over most of the faces around me. And I could feel my own face looking totally blank. "Huh?"

"Agent Zack," Sorn said, "it's time to answer the question of yours that I keep not answering."

I looked at her, my nerves as taut and tingly as an electric wire.

"Izbor is your home planet."

If it's possible to feel ice cold and burning hot at the same time, I did. No words came out of me.

Sorn continued. "Physically, Izborians look similar to Earth's humans, enough at least for minor surgery to disguise the difference. When the Galactic Union needed to plant an Alien Agent on Earth, Izbor agreed to provide one of its infants. Helping newly emerging civilizations is a cause they believe in."

That jolted me a bit. "And my . . . my parents, my real parents, didn't mind?"

"They do things differently on Izbor. Biological parents never know which offspring are theirs. But Izborians care about all their children. And they have some very powerful defensive weapons. We might be safe there."

Sorn returned to the controls where she and Vraj entered some coordinates. I felt totally stunned. Beside me, Shasta whispered, "How exciting! You'll get to see your own world."

It was exciting. Kind of scary, too. Since I'd learned I was an alien a couple of years ago, I'd often wondered what my own world was like. But that always made me feel kind of guilty. Earth seemed like my real home, and my human parents like my real family. Even now, I didn't want that to change.

You'd think that with all of this churning around in my brain, I wouldn't have been able to sleep. But it had been a really long, hard day and night on that last planet. I finally got around to changing out of my pirate costume, but I tucked the dagger in my belt, just in case. Very soon I was asleep, curled up in my chair. I didn't wake up until the stars were back and a new planet came into sight outside the viewport. My planet.

It was still far enough away to see Izbor as a ball. Beneath swirls of white stretched narrow swaths of blue-green. Probably oceans. Between these were large patches of yellow, orange, and pale green.

A bell chimed from our ship's console, and a voice was suddenly being transmitted in an alien language. The device in my ear immediately sent a translation.

"Do not proceed further. The planet Izbor wishes to minimize outside contact. Our orbital defense shield may be activated if you continue your approach. If, despite this warning, you wish to proceed, fully state your identity and your purpose. The matter will be transmitted to the Izborian Grand Council for evaluation."

"Friendly folks," Khh hissed as the transmission ended. "Is this 'orbital defense' stuff a bluff?"

"No," Sorn answered. "Test it and we'll be instantly vaporized. Like I said, they're an old civilization—they've had plenty of time to develop powerful weapons. I'll tell them what they want to know and hope they listen to reason."

She pressed a button and began speaking slowly. "This is Agent Sorn of the Galactic Union. Our ship is being pursued by ships of the Kiapa Kapa Syndicate. Their aim is to capture or kill native-born Izborian Zack

Gaither. As an infant, Zack was planted on a precontact planet where he was eventually to serve as an envoy of the Galactic Union. Your Grand Council permitted Zack to serve in this peaceful capacity. We were attempting to convey him to Galactic Union Headquarters when attacked by the Syndicate. Now we are requesting temporary sanctuary on his home planet, one known across the galaxy for its wisdom and compassion."

Time dragged on with no answer from Izbor. Waiting felt like transluminal travel all over again. I stared down at the planet outside. This place looked very different from Earth. More land, less water, and a lot less green. I also noticed a slight shimmer around it, as if an almost-invisible net enclosed the place. The defensive shield they mentioned? Not a very friendly homecoming.

Suddenly the net became very visible, a web of glowing threads with black blobs at every cross point. Then, with a quiver, a small portion of the web dissolved. The voice again filled our cabin. "Enter. A tractor beam will escort you to the proper landing point."

I got the feeling from the way Vraj was muttering that we weren't so much being escorted as being dragged. But I guess we were heading toward where we wanted to go.

And it was an awesome-looking sort of place. A sparkly blue beam of light pulled us through the opening in the defense net. Its shaft shot up from the planet's surface like a searchlight. We slid down it, over one of the narrow oceans and toward a range of pointy mountains. More than just pointy, I realized as we drew nearer. These mountains were really a vast cluster of needle-sharp spires. They definitely did not look like something you wanted to be hurtling toward at this incredible speed.

Finally I saw that the beam was shooting out of a long cleft among the spires. We dropped into it, and soon rock was sliding past us. Staring out the viewscreen, I thought I saw creatures scuttling up and down the sheer surfaces.

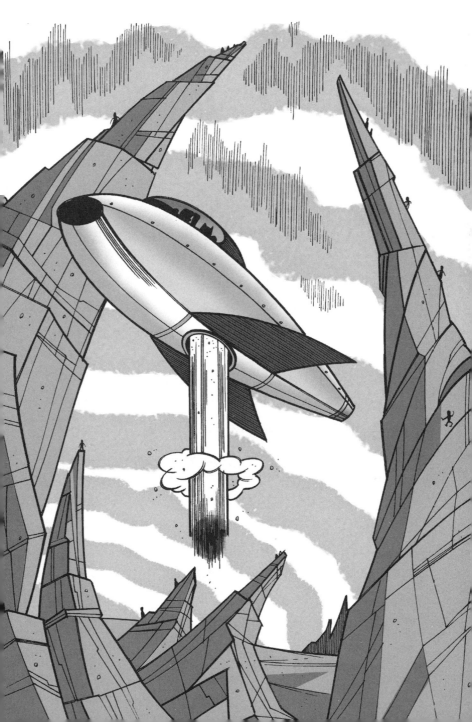

Shasta had seen them too. "What are those?" she whispered.

I stared harder. "People, I think. Human-shaped." I stopped with a gulp. My people. No wonder I was such a natural climber.

Our ship sank down and down, finally settling on a broad ledge that jutted out from the rock pillars. Through our viewscreens we saw a high, arched doorway in one of those pillars slowly open. A group of people walked toward us.

Sorn stood up and headed toward our ship's hatch. "All right, everybody; this is a diplomatic matter. Let me do the talking. I've dealt with Izborians before."

With Sorn in the lead, we trooped down the ramp. The Izborian delegation neared. I was staring so hard that I almost tripped over my own feet. They were very colorful. I don't mean their clothes, which were mostly grey tunics and short capes. I mean *them*. They were every color imaginable. Blue, green, red, pink, orange, black. Each one's hair was a different color too.

They were basically human-shaped, though. As they came closer, I saw they didn't have any ears, unless the feathers ringing their heads were ears and not decorations. Their eyes were round like an owl's, and as one raised a hand in greeting, I noticed that the hand had two thumbs. I shivered, thinking about the "minor surgery" Sorn had mentioned. Thankfully, I didn't remember any of it.

"Greetings to Galactic Agent Sorn and her party," said a bright turquoise Izborian. My translator picked up the words, but the musical quality of the voice came across by itself. "We are proud to be able to offer the sanctuary you seek and are pleased that one of our own has done well in his duties. We will take you all to a guest room for you to refresh yourselves. Later, please proceed to the meeting chamber."

The delegates turned, and we followed them through the arched doorway. Inside, high corridors branched off in every direction. The pale walls were smooth, but not totally flat, like they were made out of melted wax. We passed openings to several high-ceilinged rooms, some empty, some occupied by Izborians. One very large room we passed was full of children, mostly younger-looking than me. Some sort of school or day-care center? It rattled me to think I could have been one of them.

Our escorts left us in a good-sized room furnished with long, puffy pillows. Basins rose at different heights from the floor, dribbling water from one to the next. Tables and benches seemed to sprout out of the floor too. The best part, though, was the bowls of what looked like food on those tables.

By the time I'd finished gawking, Vraj and Khh were already seated at the table, sampling the eats. Tu was examining the basin fountains to see how they worked. Sorn and Shasta stood at one of the tall windows, looking out. I joined them.

The view was amazing. We looked into the deep cleft and the rocky pinnacles that soared above it. Dark openings dotted those pillars, and we could see colorful Izborians standing in some of them. As we watched, a few climbed up and down the rock while others launched themselves into the air and flew about. I could fly? No, they weren't flapping wings. Their short capes billowed out as the wearers coasted like people hang gliding. Except some glided upward. Cool.

Shasta seemed to agree. She punched my arm and said, "Not a bad place to be from. If you can't be from Earth, of course."

Sorn turned from the view and looked toward the table. "I trust you two are leaving some of that food for the rest of us."

"If you get over here in time," Vraj said through a mouthful of something mushy and green.

The food was good, although I didn't recognize any of it. Mostly there were curly, squiggly things and spongy round ones. I had to fight down the urge to ask what everything was. I figured that if I was going to be on alien planets for a while, I'd have to be eating a lot of alien food. I'd probably be better off not knowing what things were—in case I freaked out and starved to death.

We'd just flopped down on the big pillows after eating when another group of Izborians arrived. I think it was a mostly new group, anyway, because most of their skin tones were different.

"What color do you think you were?" Shasta whispered beside me as we followed the others through corridors again.

I shrugged but kept looking at the Izborians. The dark green of the guy in front was really handsome. But then a turquoise lady beside us smiled at me, and I decided that would be a good color too. Maybe she was my mother. The thought bothered me. No, my real mother was back on Earth. Still, I thought I'd like to at least meet my birth parents.

We were ushered into a round room. It seemed to be in the center of a tall spire. The ceiling was very high, and the walls were carved with arched windows that let in golden sunlight. It was the center of the room, though, that really grabbed my attention. Two crescent-shaped tables faced each other. The seats along the rim of one were all empty. The other had a dozen Izborians seated along it.

We were shown to empty seats and sat down, looking across at the dazzling mix of Izborian skin and hair colors. A bright red woman with lavender hair stood up at the center of their table. I thought she was one of those who had met our ship.

"Representatives of the Galactic Union and the emerging planet Earth, we are honored to offer you the requested sanctuary. We have discussed the matter and will gladly assist you in reaching Galactic Union Headquarters—untroubled by those pursuing you. But before you go, let us all enjoy a more informal visit. We of the council would be pleased to show you around our home here and speak with you about your own home worlds. I, as current council head, would particularly love to talk with the native Izborian."

She smiled, left her place, and walked toward me. "Come, Agent Zackary Gaither, let me show you our gardens."

She reached out a hand and took mine. Instead of a little finger, her hand had a second thumb. That could be pretty useful.

We walked through a tall doorway and along another corridor. This one opened to reveal sunlight and a really breathtaking garden. Waterfalls dropped in glittery veils from the sides of pointy rock pillars. They cascaded into deep pools connected by a winding silver stream. Strange plants grew everywhere. Tall, feathery blue ones fluttered in a warm breeze, and the ground was covered with tiny flowers that glowed like Christmas lights.

We followed a white stone path to a bench carved into the side of a boulder. The red lady sat and patted the seat beside her. "I'd like to show you all of Izbor, but you have a job to do, and I imagine you may have a few questions."

She was sure right about that. I was nearly exploding with questions. Which one to ask first? I looked down at our hands.

"I guess they had to make a few changes in me before they took me to Earth."

"Not many. Minor alterations to your eyes, your ears. And changing your skin color, of course."

"Yeah. What is it with the skin colors here? I mean, they're great, but everyone seems different."

She chuckled. "That was the idea. Eons and eons ago, Izborians came in only a few shades, and people of one color tended to distrust those of a different color. There were wars sometimes and lots of cruelty. When our people learned how to change the face of living things, we made it so that everyone was born a different color. That way there could be no groups of one color hating people of another color. *Everyone* was different."

I looked down at her red hand in mine. "So was I the same color . . . as my real parents?"

"Not likely. The colors appear at random."

I cleared my throat. The big question: "Do you know who my mother and father were?"

"No, nobody would. I know things are done differently on your adopted planet. Earth families are small. Here we all live as one family. The actual identity of one child's parents isn't important. The love and caring in both worlds is the same, though."

I sighed happily. It felt like a tight knot inside me had just come undone. I'd grown up on Earth and learned its ways. My mother and father there were still my family. And that seemed to be all right with the universe.

We talked for a while longer, with me telling her a lot about Earth. Eventually the sun slipped from the sky and was replaced by an incredible number of glittering stars. The red woman led me back to the guest room, where the other passengers from our ship were returning as well. Over another meal, they all jabbered on about the wonders they'd seen and heard, the music, the art, the libraries.

I didn't say much until finally Shasta poked me. "So what did you learn about you and this place? You want to move back?"

With a chuckle I shook my head. "It's like what Dorothy said about Kansas."

She clicked her heels. "There's no place like home."

CHAPTER SIX

Those big floor pillows made good beds. When we all lurched awake in the morning, there was more food on our table. Then two Izborians showed up and took us to a room none of us had seen before. We got there by a sort of elevator. Not like an Earth elevator, because there was no floor or anything. You just stepped into a big, hollow tube and gently floated down, down, down.

From there we stepped into a large, round room with no windows. There were monitor screens all along the walls. Tu was the first to figure out what they were showing.

"Looks like different views of Izbor from space."

"Right," Sorn said. "And that cluster of lights must be Syndicate ships waiting for us."

"Like cats outside a mouse hole," Shasta added.

"I'm not sure what cats or mouse holes are," said the red woman, "but you'll have no trouble getting away. That's why we brought you here. To show you."

She gestured around the darkened room. The only light came from the screens and from a glowing red ball in the center of the floor. By that dim glow I could make out three Izborians seated on benches circling the ball.

"This is one of the places where we channel energy," the dark green Izborian said. "Mostly we focus on defense here."

Iv and Tu had been closely examining the room. "I don't see any mechanisms here other than the screens," Iv said. "Is the red globe a weapon?"

"No, an energy source linked to the core of our planet," the green man explained. "Our minds use it to create the protective shield around Izbor and fend off troublemakers."

"Your minds? Cool!" Shasta said. "I've seen Zack do stuff like that."

"But not defend a whole planet!" I objected. "Just small stuff. And I don't really know how I do it."

The green man smiled. "You'll grow into it. It's a natural Izborian ability, and Agent Sorn tells me you've been training."

All that was mind-blowing enough. But it was totally awesome when the three seated Izborians closed their eyes and held out their hands to the red globe. Almost immediately, the screens showed the energy net around the planet beginning to glow. It surged outward, pushing the Syndicate ships away like driftwood on a giant tidal wave.

"Time you got back onto your ship and left," the red lady said. "You should have plenty of time to safely reach Galactic Union Headquarters before your enemies regroup. Our energy shield does not push softly."

After hurried farewells, we left my birth planet. Then came more of that odd timeless time. I used it to think more about where I had just been. Izbor was full of wonders, I thought, but not really home. After I don't know how long, we popped out again in real space and saw the amazing sight of the Galactic Union Headquarters.

I was expecting a planet, but this looked like a huge space station. Odd-shaped metal bits poked out everywhere. That makes it sound like a heap of space junk, but it was really beautiful, spangled with light, floating in the blackness of space.

"Wow," was my clever comment.

"Double wow," Shasta said, staring out the viewscreen beside me.

Tu gave an excited whistle. "I've never seen this place before. Heard a lot about it, though. My father used to hang out with the guy who later got elected president of the galaxy. He never talks much about those days."

Just then Iv placed a slim, four-fingered hand on his son's shoulder. "For good reason. Gifalkapul and I were rather wild youth. We managed to get into a good deal of trouble— an example I do not want you to follow. Good old Gif . . ." He walked away, chuckling.

We would have spent time wondering about what kind of trouble he and his friend had gotten into, but the view sucked up our attention. Various spaceships moved to and from the floating headquarters, like bees around a giant flower.

After a minute, Shasta spoke. "Incredibly cool. But all those things don't really look like my idea of spaceships. Like that one." She giggled as a flat yellow square with holes zoomed by.

"Right," I admitted. "Looks more like extra-terrestrial Swiss cheese. And how about that one? It's like a giant wad of crumpled paper."

Tu pointed to a long spiky ship. "At home we have a fruit, a gub gub, which looks like that one."

"No," I said, "I'd say it's a cross between a hot dog and a porcupine."

Sorn had walked up behind us. "We'll be docking soon. I've informed the president of the Galactic Union of our arrival. But otherwise, we'll want to keep a low profile until the council meeting. That won't be for a day or more. So you'll have a chance to explore the place a little on your own if you want."

If I wanted? I could be back home, going to school as usual, or I could be exploring a gigantic space station full of amazing aliens. Not exactly a tough choice.

Shasta and Tu felt the same way. After we'd landed and settled into our quarters (which were pretty amazing themselves), Sorn, Khh, and Vraj, as Galactic Patrol agents, had official duties to tend to, and Iv said he had old friends to visit. So, armed with a holographic guidebook and cautioned not to get into trouble, we three kids set off to explore.

I'd liked to have been able to act like a cool Alien Agent, like I hung out in places like this all the time. But no way could I pull that off. The whole place was mind-boggling: high hallways; vast rooms; escalator-like things that went up, down, and around in spirals. But it was all the aliens wandering about that had us staring like tourists. I kept thinking that I wished Ken could see this.

Some of the aliens were so large that you had to scurry to keep from being stepped on. Others were so small, you had to worry about stepping on them. Some flew, some slithered, some bounced. They came with any number of legs or tentacles, heads, hands, and eyes. Some glanced at us curiously. We were aliens to them. In fact, I realized, everyone in this huge building was an "alien." We all looked equally weird to somebody.

The translator in my ear was practically overheating, it was working so hard to translate the scraps of language it picked up. We walked around (or rode moving sidewalks), visiting a vast library, a museum, gift shops, and restaurants. The floating smells made us realize how hungry we all were.

Inside, tables hovered at different heights in the air. Chairs of all different shapes floated about. We picked three that seemed to fit us and herded them toward one of the empty tables. As we sat, a menu suddenly popped out of the tabletop. I frowned at it. Our translators worked on spoken language but not on written words. Tu, though, was a one-hundred-year-old kid with lots of schooling, and he pressed buttons for things he could eat and ones he figured Shasta and I could handle. Our tabletop glowed, and almost instantly there was food in front of us.

Tu got a bowl of orange artichoke-looking things, while Shasta and I each had plates of what looked like muddy potato chips and bright pink spaghetti. Once I got up the courage to try my stuff, it wasn't bad. Well, not too bad. Imagine peppermint-flavored spinach or liver marinated in maple syrup.

We were just finishing when I looked up and gasped. An alien was coming toward us, an alien who looked oddly familiar. I poked Shasta and whispered, "Fairy."

The pale green girl was maybe two feet high and looked basically human except for the pointy ears—and the wings. She giggled musically when she saw us staring and fluttered over to the middle of our table.

"You must be the Earth people I heard were coming. Welcome!"

"Uh . . . yes . . . thank you," I stammered. Somehow it's easier to talk with weird-looking aliens than with something out of a fairy tale that you never imagined was real.

"I've always wanted to meet humans." She sat down and threw us a dazzling smile. "But only one of you is a native, right?"

I nodded. "Shasta here is the actual Earth person, but I grew up on the planet."

The little thing clapped her hands excitedly. "Wonderful! My friends and I have been learning about Earth. It's all the rage now. We'd just *love* to talk with you about the place. Won't you came and meet my friends? They'll be *so excited!*"

She fluttered up into the air and off toward a doorway, beckoning us to follow.

We three looked at each other. "I've never seen anyone of her species before," Tu said. "I wonder where she's from."

"I have a feeling some of her ancestors might have hung out on Earth for a while," I commented.

"So, let's go ask!" Shasta said, slipping off her floating chair. Tu and I did the same, and we all followed the fairy flitting through the air in front of us.

The last few days had been jam-packed with oddness, but somehow this took first prize. She led us through a maze of corridors, tunnels, and moving walkways. Tu and I took turns fumbling with our guidebook, but soon we felt hopelessly lost. Rounding a corner, we suddenly stepped into nothingness. But instead of falling, we floated slowly down a round shaft that looked like a giant, glowing green Slinky.

We dropped out onto a carpet of bouncy, multicolored bubbles. Tu, Shasta, and I stumbled to our feet, trying to keep our guide in sight. Rounding another corner, we saw her standing ahead of us, giggling and pointing to a blank wall. She touched it, and a round doorway opened, letting out a wave of light and twinkly music. She slipped through, and after a moment we did too.

The room wasn't large, but it had a very tall ceiling and was crowded. I glanced around at our fairy's friends. A couple looked like her. One looked like a walking celery stalk, and another like a fat, two-headed squirrel.

"Well, here he is," the fairy said. Her giggle sounded oddly nasty. And were those fangs in her sweet little mouth? A couple of tall creatures that looked like Mr. Potato Head stepped aside and someone else stepped forward. Someone unpleasantly familiar.

A smile spread over the Gnairt's bloated face. "Well, well, Agent Zack Gaither. Got you at last!"

CHapTer SeveN

I grabbed Tu and Shasta by the shoulders and yanked them back. But the door had snapped shut behind us. The creatures closed in. A yodeling screech came from above. Several giant centipede-like things dropped down from high windows.

Everything got crazy, fast. Everyone was grabbing at us. We kicked and hit whatever we could reach. The yelling and squeaking and bellowing were awful. Suddenly I was yanked upward in a mess of sticky thread.

Centipedes have always creeped me out, and I'm talking about the little wriggly ones under stones. This guy was as long as an alligator and just as cuddly. It and two others scrabbled up the walls with me, Shasta, and Tu wrapped like flies meant for a spider's dinner. Below us, the other creatures whooped and screeched even louder.

The sounds faded as our captors slithered through dark openings in the wall and along a maze of twisty passages. I tried to scream, to move, or just get a better view of where we were going. But the threads that first snagged me spread until I was nearly wrapped like a mummy. It occurred to me that my career as an important Alien Agent was about to come to a sticky, painful end.

Though I could hardly see, I felt us scuttling sideways, and then up, then down, then up and down again. Finally there was light, and I rolled across the hard floor like a dropped pencil. The centipedes chattered about something that I couldn't make out through the silky stuff. I could only see a large blue shape standing over me. There was a sizzling noise, and the threads binding me snapped, curled, and vanished like smoke.

Struggling to stand, I stared up at an eight-foot-high blue mop. Well, mop head. Thick blue cords hung down all around it. If it had a mouth or eyes or anything, I couldn't see them. A voice buzzed from somewhere inside it.

"Sorry if my guardsmen were a little rough. I ordered them to follow you, keep you safe, and bring you here if you got into any trouble. Apparently you did. Kiapa Kapa Syndicate trouble."

Beside me, Shasta and Tu were getting to their feet. Tu looked at the blue mop and gasped. "President Gifalkapul!"

The guy laughed, and his blue mop strands jiggled. "Well met, young Tu. My good friend, your father, visited me earlier and told me you young people were off exploring. There's been some feuding over Earth's membership nomination, and I assured him before he set off that I would have you guarded."

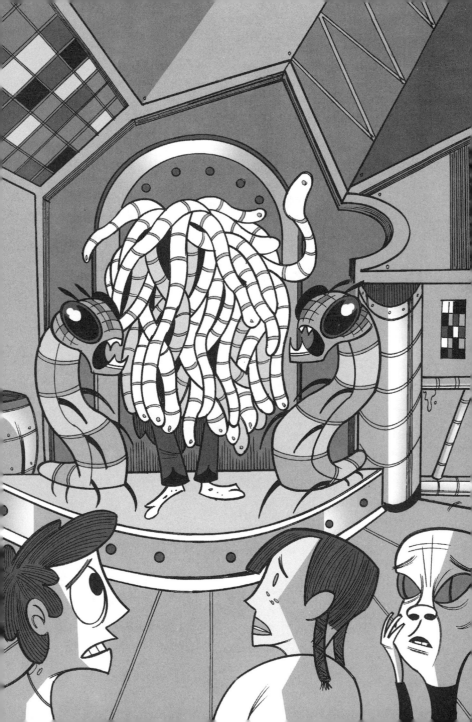

With that, he waved some mop strands toward the three giant centipedes who were lounging at the side of the room. "Well done, boys. I think I can keep them safe from here."

I tried not to shudder as the three rose, bowed their segmented bodies, and scuttled out a door.

"Now, let me formally greet you," the Galactic President said. "Zack Gaither, it is a pleasure to meet such an accomplished young agent." He grabbed my hand with one of his mop strands. Its surface was covered with little beads that tingled where I touched them, beads that looked like eyes.

"And you," he said, shaking Shasta's hand in the same way, "a gifted native of the planet Earth. I hope to soon welcome you into our galactic community and get to know all your people better.

"And Tu, son of my old troublemaking friend. It seems you are following in your father's adventurous path. I trust he has not related too many of our exploits. It would not be good for our dignified images." He didn't just shake Tu's hand. The president engulfed him in a hug that had Tu almost disappearing into a mop-strand cascade.

I looked around the room we were in. Not very impressive for the president of the Galactic Union's office. Gifalkapul must have noticed, though I wasn't sure how he could see. Maybe those beads on his mop strands really were eyes.

"This isn't my official office, Agent Zack. It's where I go when I want to get away from things official. And what I have to tell you isn't strictly official. I have studied all the information we have about planet Earth, and there is a great deal of it. It is my personal opinion that the planet is worthy to join the Galactic Union. But I am elected by the council and must abide by their wishes. Those wishes will be determined at an upcoming assembly. However, there are those who, for reasons of their own, will try to prevent membership from being offered. It seems they will stop at nothing to accomplish this, as your near-abduction shows."

"That and everything else that's been going on," I added. "But I still don't understand why Earth is so important to them. I mean, I love the place. It feels like my real home. But I bet the galaxy is full of great planets."

"It is. But Earth is on the fringe of the area we can easily protect. It has great natural resources, and we suspect that its natives have some untapped abilities which criminals might like to control. The Kiapa Kapa have members from many species, so it is not easy to know who to trust. My advice now to you three is to go back to your quarters and stay there until the council assembly. It will be in only a few of your days, and there should be plenty in your quarters to entertain you."

I'm sure there was. I'd already seen what looked like a massive entertainment center in one room. But it was another room that it had that interested me now. And it didn't feel like we'd get there soon enough.

"Uh, thank you, Your...Honor, Your Presidentship. But before we go, do you have . . . I mean is there someplace, someplace nearby, where people can . . . "

Gifalkapul bubbled what was probably a laugh. "Down that corridor is a relief station, designed for many species and their needs. Is that what you wish?"

I nodded awkwardly, wondering if he'd read my mind. Probably just my body language. It had been hours since we'd been near a bathroom, and I guess I was kind of squirmy.

Gifalkapul told us that when we'd finished, he'd send us back with an escort of his centipede guards. That idea made me a different kind of squirmy, but I gratefully headed toward the bathroom. The hallway wound around to a large, weird "relief station." When you think about aliens, you don't usually think about the different ways that they go to the bathroom. I wasn't sure I wanted to meet the folks who used some of these facilities.

Modestly, Shasta, Tu, and I went our separate ways. When we'd finished our business, we met up at the room's main door. "Thanks for asking," Shasta said to me. "I didn't know how to bring that up either."

I was about to answer when we heard noise back down the hall. It sounded like President Gifalkapul was arguing with someone. Or maybe he was just talking to a galactic official in his more formal voice. It was too far away for my translator to kick in, but in a moment, the voices stopped and we slowly walked back down the hall.

The president was alone when we got there. "It has been an honor meeting you three," he said. "Now, several of my guard will escort you to the guest quarters." He shook my hand with a mop strand, then Shasta's, then Tu's.

As Gifalkapul pointed us to the office's main door, Tu halted. "Wait, let's go back to the bathroom. I think I left the guidebook there. You two can help me look for it."

With that, Tu scurried back into the hallway we'd just come down. Shasta and I shrugged and followed. But Tu passed the relief station door and turned another corner.

Confused, we did the same and found him staring at us with eyes wider than usual and flapping his grey hands. "It's not him!"

"Who's not him?" I asked.

"I don't know who he *is*, but he's not him!"

"Who?"

"Him! Gifalkapul. That guy in the office isn't him."

"But we just . . . " Shasta began.

"No, we first met the real president. But when we were away, this new guy was substituted for him."

"How do you know?"

"My species can bond with people. My dad and Gifalkapul were very close. When he first hugged me, I felt that bond, kind of soaked it up. The person who just shook my hand is someone else."

Remembering the raised voices we'd heard, I nodded. "Then the real president's . . ."

"Been abducted!" Shasta finished. "We'd better not go back and let *this* guy's creepy guards escort us anywhere."

I shuddered. That's for sure. Not only would they be giant centipedes. They'd be bad-guy giant centipedes.

CHAPTER EIGHT

Tu pulled the guidebook out of his side pack. He'd had it all along. "Right. No going back there." He seemed focused on the thing. But his eyes were closed.

"These guys won't stop at much, will they?" I said, thinking how close we'd come to falling into their trap again. "So we'd better find where they took the real Gifalkapul."

"How can *we* do that?" Shasta asked as she and I took off after Tu. He was charging down the hallway in the other direction. "Shouldn't we report this to somebody?"

"No time," Tu answered. "Like I said, we've bonded. But the bond's not very deep yet, so we've got to hurry. They took him in this general direction. Hmm. Then headed right. And now up slightly."

We trotted along a maze of mostly deserted corridors and the occasional kitchen or equipment storeroom. Tu seemed to be following some internal guide, so I took the guidebook from him and tried to figure out where we were going.

Shasta read over my shoulder as we jogged along. "Looks like we're heading to some sort of airport . . . or spaceport, I guess."

"Makes sense," I said. "But if the kidnappers get the real president onto a spaceship, we won't be able to follow. They've probably got really good defenses against stowaways."

"He's right, Tu," Shasta called. "Let's alert someone now, so they can keep the ship from taking off."

Tu had stopped where the corridor we were in led into an enormous open space. "Except, I don't think they're taking him to a ship," he said, eyes closed again. "At least not right away. They're in the middle of this zone all right, but heading down."

The area we stepped into was very high-ceilinged. In fact, it didn't look like it had a ceiling at all—black space and scattered stars stretched above us. I realized it was a clear dome. They'd had something like that in the smaller spaceport where we'd landed. In the center of the room was a huge, clear tube rising from floor to ceiling. Inside the tube were columns of different heights, many of which cradled spaceships. Some of those ships were really enormous—like that one that flies overhead at the beginning of the first *Star Wars* movie. Only this was real.

Shasta poked me, and I realized I was just standing there gawking. We took off after Tu again. He wove his way through the aliens walking to and fro across the floor, its tiles changing color as waves of rainbow light flowed through them. The people and machines we passed were carrying all kinds of cargo. I realized it would have been easy for several someones to carry the blue-mop president through this crowd if he was wrapped up.

We'd nearly reached the giant spaceship enclosure when Tu stopped and stared at a cluster of large, multicolored tubes that rose up about twenty feet from the floor. They all had large openings in them. Tu walked around them like a dog sniffing for a scent. He stopped at a purple tube.

"They took him down here," he whispered. "Better follow before he gets too far away and I lose touch."

That made sense, but I sure didn't like the idea of creeping around the bowels of a giant space station where enemies looked like sweet little fairies and friends looked like gross centipedes. I liked it even less after we stepped through the tube's opening and found it was another elevator shaft—with no floor. Some sort of force wrapped around us like a dark blanket and swiftly yanked us down. There weren't even any buttons to press for what floor we wanted. It wasn't nearly as gentle as the lifts on Izbor. But either one would take a lot of getting used to.

We went down, and down, and down, until I didn't think we'd ever reach bottom. Suddenly we jolted to a stop. The three of us toppled over each other, practically rolling out another dark opening into a dimly lit room. I looked up fearfully, expecting to see nasty faces staring down at us. No one was there.

Tu was already up and hurrying down a tunnel lit by faintly glowing bands of purple and orange. We followed as it went down in an ever-tightening spiral into another corridor. The rough, black walls were lit even more dimly by splotches of yellow crystal.

Tu was leading us more slowly now, muttering as he went. The sickly yellow glow ahead began to fade as a blue-white light sifted down the corridor. With this light, we could see that the walls around us were not metal or anything else artificial. They were rock, like we were in some deep coal mine.

"I thought this was a man-made—*creature*-made—space station," I whispered to Shasta.

"I was flipping through the guidebook while we were eating at that weird restaurant," she whispered back. "Apparently the core of the place is a long-dead planetoid whose star has died. No species claimed it, so it was a neutral place to build Galactic Union Headquarters. That was a really long time ago, and the place has grown a lot since."

No kidding, I thought, but then I forgot the rock and stared at the source of the blue-white light. Our corridor ended at the base of a huge machine that looked like a pulsing crystal wrapped in wire. The wires connected to a network of crisscrossing pipes and machinery. The tall space around it vibrated with a steady humming.

We stood staring at the pulsing light. "Wow," I finally managed. "Must be some sort of energy source."

"I hope it's not radiating something that's going to kill us," Shasta said.

Tu shrugged. "It's wrecking our search, though. Whatever it's radiating is jamming the trail I've been following. I have no idea where they've got Gifalkapul now."

Bad, I thought. But the trail had led him this far. "Maybe if we walk around this thing, you'll pick it up again."

"In any case, let's move," Shasta said. "Some bit of machinery is leaking on me!" I turned to see her trying to brush a blot of yellowish slime from her shoulder. Just then a big blob of the stuff landed on my head. I looked up.

Stretched ten feet along a pipe above my head was one of the ugliest things I'd seen in a universe full of ugly things. It was long and yellow, with wiggly eye-stalks, horns, and wings. That might sound kind of cool, like a dragon. But no, it looked like a giant, ugly, flying slug.

Is this one of those nasty-looking things that really turns out to be a good guy, I wondered?

Nope.

CHAPTER NINE

Flaps opened on the slug-thing's sides. Long sheets of slime dropped down and slapped against the three of us. Suddenly we were stuck to the sheets like flies on flypaper. With wet flapping sounds, the thing took off, dragging us through the air beneath it. We were swung around to the far side of the crystal machine and into a narrow corridor carved from the same black rock.

"This would be a good time to do something clever and alien," Shasta called to me as we sailed along, bouncing painfully against the rock walls.

Right. But what? I wondered. I still haven't figured out all I can do or how to do it. Usually I need some power source to redirect with my mind. I didn't dare mess with the machine behind us, for fear of blowing up something important. Like me, Shasta, and Tu. My watch battery worked before, but if I tried to shoot at the creature that was carrying us, the power might just as easily travel down the slime sheets and fry us as well.

The question solved itself when all three sheets suddenly slid back into the slug's sides and we dropped down to the cold, hard floor. When I got my breath back, I sat up and found myself staring at a pair of Gnairt. Between them was a round something that looked like it came from a tide pool—except that it was big as a truck tire and had a nasty beak and four bulgy eyes in the middle of a circle of waving pink tentacles.

"Ah," said one of the Gnairt.

"Ah, a ha ha ha," the other Gnairt added in a voice like a plugged-up drain. "Some of the pro-Earth delegation. And the planted agent! Excellent. Now practically no one will be able to present Earth's case."

The pink-tentacle guy rasped, "They might hold useful information, but there's no time to question them now."

"So let's kill them!" said the second Gnairt, sounding all too happy about it.

"No, fool, imprison them!" tide-pool guy snapped. "They might be useful when the Syndicate takes over their planet."

Good time to run, I thought. Tu and Shasta had the same thought, but we hadn't taken more than five steps when the flying slug's long tail smacked into us like a giant golf club and rolled us across the floor. Into a hole. A dark, cold, and very deep hole.

We landed in a heap. After much groaning, we sorted ourselves out and decided nothing important was broken. But that was all done by feel. It was dark as a tomb in that hole. Not a comforting comparison.

"Okay," Shasta's voice sounded from the blackness beside me. "This would be an even better time to do something clever and alien."

I grunted and looked up the shaft of our deep hole. At the top—*way* at the top—was a round opening, a circle of grey light crossed by a grid of bars. I could think of one alien thing to do. Not clever, but possibly useful.

I climbed. Trying not to think how impossible this was, I found foot- and hand-holds in the rough rock walls and steadily made my way up. Finally I was splayed like a lizard just under the grid. I could hear the Gnairt and the tide-pool thing talking a few feet away.

"Having them all out of the way will destroy Earth's chances," said one of the Gnairt.

The other one bubbled a laugh. "And having the Galactic President on our side will cinch it for us. Earth will be firmly in the Syndicate's hands in no time."

"Speaking of time, you've babbled away enough of it," the other voice wheezed. "It is time we returned to the others. All four prisoners are secure, and we need to ready ourselves for the council debate."

Their bickering got farther and farther away. From the sound of wet flapping, it seemed that the flying slug was leaving as well. I waited several minutes, then grabbed hold of the metal grate over my head with one hand.

It was like one of those cartoons where someone pokes a light socket. Lightning zapped all around me and my hair stood on end. Also, I screamed.

Yanking my hand free, I hung by my one good hand to the rock wall, whimpering. I know, Alien Agents probably aren't supposed to whimper, but that *hurt*.

Shasta's worried voice called from below. "Zack, you okay?"

"Yeah, just fine."

It was too dark to see, but I imagined my hand looked like an overdone hamburger. I concentrated on the self-healing thing. Another alien skill I had finally mastered. But getting out of this hole would be something else.

Focusing my mind on the little wristwatch battery, I tried to direct a small spear of energy toward the metal grate. All it did was bounce off in a shower of sparks. Some sort of force field, maybe. Wishing I'd spent more time on my agent lessons, I climbed slowly back down the wall.

With my feet on the stone floor again, I started explaining what had happened, but Tu shushed me.

"Quiet. She's speaking to someone."

Who else was down here? Surely not that large mop, Gifalkapul, or our landing would have been a lot softer.

I stared into the dark but couldn't see a thing. Wait, maybe a fuzzy glowing spot. I could only glimpse it out of the corner of my eye, not by looking at it directly. Shasta was mumbling in a language I didn't know, but it was too soft for my translator to pick up.

Were we all going crazy being cooped up down here? Me seeing things that weren't there, and Shasta talking to them? I just sat and waited quietly, not too eager to learn the answer.

I'd almost fallen asleep when Shasta's voice cut into my nasty half-dreams. Though not many nightmares could be worse than what was really going on. Trapped in the dark and about to totally fail as an Alien Agent.

"They don't normally bother with what's going on above," Shasta said. "But they think it's kind of nice talking with someone after a bunch of centuries. So they'll help us get out."

"Who's 'they'?" Tu and I asked at the same time.

"I guess all worlds do have spirits. The living creatures on this world died millennia ago. There's just this cold rock core left. But its spirits are hanging on."

"Whoa," I breathed. "Talk about clever alien powers."

"Yeah, it kind of freaks me out too. But I think maybe it's something all humans could do if we really tried."

"So what did they say about us getting out of here?" Tu's voice said in the dark. He sounded pretty cold, like his teeth would be chattering if he had teeth.

"They said that this rock is honeycombed with holes and tunnels. Some lead up and out. We just have to break through to them."

"And they can help us do that?" Tu asked.

"I don't think so. They haven't much in the way of bodies."

Tu groaned, but I was already tapping my watch. Hopefully that awful force field didn't go lower than the grate up top. I'd never found this mind-focusing thing to be easy when I was practicing in my backyard. But I had lots of reasons now to get it right. Wrapping my mind around the energy in the watch battery, I molded it into kind of a laser torch and jabbed it at the rocky floor.

Gritty dust exploded in our faces. We coughed and wheezed, but I kept cutting. Suddenly the whole floor gave way and we tumbled downward. Luckily it wasn't very far down. I was really getting tired of dropping into dark, cold, rocky pits.

When we scrambled to our knees and started feeling around, we realized this wasn't another pit at all. Was it a tunnel? Squinting, I could half-see a glint of light to our right. It jiggled back and forth, like it wanted our attention. A spirit guide? We crawled that way and then cautiously stood up. The tunnel was just high enough so we didn't have to walk hunched over like cave people.

Shasta took the lead as we followed the barely visible light through a maze of tunnels and gouges in the rock. We passed lots of pits and side tunnels, and I was really glad we had a guide who seemed to know where it was going. When the way started to lead upward, the light spun around Shasta's head for a moment and then vanished. We were left in total darkness.

"I guess we're on our own now," she said.

"What if we meet more crossroads?" I asked.

"Maybe I can take it from here," Tu said. "I'm picking up a trace of that bond again."

"And for light," Shasta offered, "why don't you light up something with your watch?"

I hadn't thought of that. Maybe I could make a light. "I think my battery's low."

"Try mine." She waved her arm toward me and ended up swatting me in the face. I grabbed around for Shasta's watch and reached her hand. Her palm felt nice—all warm and dry. I squeezed it and was suddenly glad that the darkness hid my red face.

Fumbling for her watch, I mentally probed inside it and pulled out some light energy. It wavered in my hand. I knelt, groping around for something to transfer the light to. I picked up a chunk of glassy rock and sent the light into it. It glowed like a flashlight inside a tinted soda bottle.

With our faint torch, we followed Tu. Every time we came to an intersection, Tu would stop still like he was listening to something. Then he'd choose a route. After a while, our passage narrowed. We noticed another light seeping through a slit in the rock wall ahead.

I stuck my head in the cleft and then quickly pulled back. More cautiously, I looked again.

On the other side of the rock wall, a big room had been carved from the rock. It looked empty except for what might be computer consoles. No—there was something more. A large net hung from the ceiling, and in it lay a big, shaggy blue shape.

"President Gifalkapul!" Tu cried as he squeezed out ahead of me.

The translated voice buzzed in my ear as Shasta and I squeezed through the opening. "You three! How did you find me? However did . . . Watch out for the jibjibs!"

I looked around nervously. I didn't see anything that could be a dangerous jibjib. There was only the computer-like thing on a desk with some odd-shaped chairs around it. Glowing globes on the ceiling gave off a misty light, and in one corner was a pile of what looked like jelly beans.

"How can we get you down?" Tu asked as he walked toward the computer.

"Don't try to touch the net until you turn off the force field," Gifalkapul warned. I looked at my own burned hand. Instead of black and charred, it was turning a shiny pink. Nearly healed. That's one useful alien power.

Tu was studying the computer, though from over his shoulder it looked far too alien for me. Suddenly, Shasta screamed behind us.

"Jibjibs!"

CHAPTER TEN

"What are jibjibs?" I asked, turning around. The answer came in a cloud of hopping, squealing, biting jelly beans. They all had four feet and lots of teeth. Needle-sharp teeth!

Soon we were three yelping blobs of nasty, colorful jelly beans. Frantically, Tu tried to brush them off his face and keep examining the computer. He jabbed at several buttons. A high hum filled the room. The hanging net trembled and then plopped on the floor behind us. The carpet of jibjibs under it suddenly fizzed and popped.

The ones that covered us fell off like rain and

lay still. They all must have been connected somehow, like Christmas tree lights.

"Yeow!" cried the suddenly free Galactic President. His mop strands were sticking out in all directions. Frantically, he leaped into the air, cleared the still-crackling net, and landed on the floor ten feet away.

"Thanks," he said weakly. "I think."

"Are you hurt?" Tu asked anxiously.

"Not permanently. Now, we need to get to the council chambers as quickly as possible. Their plot mustn't succeed."

"I'll see if I can get a message through to someone," Tu said, examining the computer again. "They don't seem to have thought to lock it down. Agent Sorn gave me a code for reaching her. Not sure I can use it through this machine, though, or do it without alerting the bad guys."

My skin was still burning from jibjib bites. I turned to Shasta. "You okay?"

"Probably, but I don't want to see a jelly bean ever again."

I nodded. "And it used to be just the green ones that I hated."

Gifalkapul shuffled toward us. "I'm amazed you three were able to track me down. The switch was accomplished so quickly, I didn't think anyone knew I was gone."

I smiled. It's not often you get complimented by the president of the galaxy. "Tu noticed the switch and was able to follow your mental trail or whatever. And Shasta has got some abilities that maybe all humans have—talking to the spirits of places. The rock core of this place still has some. I didn't do much besides zap a few things that needed zapping."

Gifalkapul made the wheezing sound I guessed was a laugh. "Well, you're quite a team. But now, if our side isn't going to lose this game, we need to go."

I eyed the crack in the rock that we'd crawled through. "I'm not sure, Your, uh, Presidentship, that you can fit in the tunnels we took."

"No need. My captors took another route. I think I can retrace it. I have a strong sense of direction."

He certainly seemed to, since he led us confidently through a maze of passages and rooms, some empty, some full of cartons and machinery.

"What is all this?" Tu asked as we hurried to keep up with the president.

"Remnants of early headquarters facilities. This space is mostly abandoned now, or used for storage, though some of the old power stations still work."

It seemed like we'd been walking for hours when we came across one of the old power stations he'd mentioned. It was the same tall, wire-wrapped crystal we'd seen earlier, still pulsing with blue-white light and humming gently.

"Ah, I know where we are now," Gifalkapul said, pointing at a doorway we hadn't taken before. "It'll be quicker to go that way, through one of the ancient council chambers. I came here once to dedicate a historic plaque."

The room was large and lit by hazy floating lights. Seats and desks of varied sizes and designs were carved from the rock. They formed rough circles around a center platform. "When the Galactic Union was first formed, some millennia ago," Gifalkapul said, "it was a lot smaller. Representatives of member planets met here. The present council space is a great deal bigger—and more comfortable. Most species don't care for stone seats."

He broke into another wheezy laugh that suddenly turned into a yelp. I stopped gazing around like a tourist and turned to him. Several presidential mop strands pointed across the wide chambers. A lot of wild-looking aliens were entering through a distant doorway, and they didn't appear to be the ghosts of space diplomats past.

"Good guys or bad guys?" Shasta whispered.

Hard to tell, I thought, until I saw a pair of Gnairt among the dozen species. I haven't met a good Gnairt yet.

"Run!" Gifalkapul yelled at us. "They probably won't kill me. They might kill you."

Running sounded like a good choice. But not the best one. Shasta, Tu, and I looked at each other and shook our heads. *Can't just run off and let the Galactic President be recaptured by a bunch of creepy thugs,* I thought.

Of course, they were *armed* creepy thugs. And we didn't even have rocks to throw. I thought of the big power crystal outside the nearby door to the chambers, but wasn't sure I could do anything that wouldn't incinerate us all.

My hand dropped to the dagger in my belt. I could have laughed. Right. Fight off a horde of enemy aliens with a fancy letter opener. Then I thought again about the power crystal. Before I could talk myself out of it, I drew the dagger and pointed it toward the glow outside the doorway. My thoughts shot from the dagger point, snaking around the doorway to the crystal's surface.

With caution, I mentally felt over it. I didn't want to tap its deep energy, just some of its surface glow.

I got more than I hoped for. Glowing power swirled into the ancient chambers and leapt in an arc toward the dagger. The blade lit up with throbbing energy, almost knocking me off my feet. More afraid of my weapon than of the enemy, I let out a wild commando yell and leaped forward.

I waved the glowing dagger like mad in the air. With every flourish, it loosed a shower of liquid energy. Where each drop fell, a column of pulsing power flared up, wavering and coiling like tall, angry flames.

The horde rushing toward us stumbled to a halt. I didn't know if this fence of energy torches would be any real protection, but they couldn't know that either. It might at least buy us time.

"Run with us, Mister President!" Tu yelled, tugging on a mop strand. Shasta joined him, and so did I, once I'd thrust my only slightly glowing dagger back into my belt.

Gifalkapul let us drag him along for a bit, then yelped again and pointed loose mop strands back across the great room. I spun around, expecting to see my flames shriveling and the horde advancing. The flares were dimming, but that wasn't the issue. Another equally wild bunch of aliens rushed through a different door. I recognized a few in this batch too. Definitely good guys!

The two groups met like crashing waves in the center of the chamber. Screams, thuds, and curses filled the air. The alien curses nearly fried my translator. As weapons fire took over, Gifalkapul broke away from us and started marching toward the fight. Shasta, Tu, and I lunged after him, each grabbing another mop strand and looking around for somewhere to drag him to safety.

Suddenly Sorn and Iv were beside us, tugging the president behind a stout pillar. "Good work, guys!" Sorn said. The smile on her purple face matched that on Iv's grey one. "We'll take care of this part. *You* get to the council chambers. The meeting's begun."

"But we can't leave . . . " I began, but was interrupted as a young dinosaur grabbed me and tossed me over her back.

"Oh, yes, you can," Vraj snarled. "Khh, take the girl."

Shasta squealed as the flying cat clamped claws on her shoulders and lifted her into the air.

Tu grabbed Iv's waist and yelled to us, "You two go and speak for your planet. I'm staying to fight with my dad."

Then we were off, Shasta soaring through the air and me hanging upside down, bouncing like a sack against Vraj's scaly back. "Okay, I'm going," I yelled. "But let me walk already!"

"Nope. Faster this way." I think Vraj enjoys tormenting me.

We dashed through doorways, along corridors, up ramps, and finally into one of those lift tubes. The tube opened onto a big plaza that looked like a giant shopping mall, with shops and stalls selling souvenirs, clothes, food—some of which smelled mouthwatering-ly good, some like things dragged from sewers.

"Down you go," Vraj hissed, plunking me back on my feet. "Walk quickly, but don't run. The Syndicate's agents could be anywhere. We mustn't call attention to ourselves."

Shasta landed with a thump beside me and started rubbing her shoulders. "That was fun, except for the claws."

I just grunted.

Like happy space tourists we strolled, swiftly, through crowds and past shops. Vraj abruptly pushed us into one particular space. A laundry center, it looked like, judging by the clothes of all shapes and sizes hanging about. With all the outlandish clothes everyone wore, if I'd decided to keep my pirate costume on I wouldn't have looked remotely out of place. Vraj flashed some sort of identification to a laundry worker, and we were shown into a back room.

"You two get into these baskets," Vraj hissed. He pushed a couple of floating baskets through the air toward us. Shasta and I pulled them down to the floor and awkwardly crawled in. Immediately they popped into the air again, just as Khh flew by, dropping in an armload of what I recognized as Galactic Patrol uniforms into Shasta's basket. Vraj piled another bunch on top of me.

The dinosaur chuckled annoyingly, grabbing hold of one basket as Khh took the other. "Now, off to make your grand entrance into the Galactic Union council chambers."

Right, I thought. *Years of training, dangerous assignments, harrowing escapes, all leading to this moment. An honored envoy of the planet Earth. Arriving in a laundry basket.*

At least it wasn't dirty laundry. Some aliens smell pretty bad.

CHAPTER ELEVEN

I can't describe the next part very well. I was under a bunch of laundry, so I couldn't see a thing, and sounds were muffled. But it seemed like we walked and stopped, walked and stopped, like we were going through a lot of security checkpoints. Made sense since this was a big-time VIP meeting. Vraj's and Khh's credentials must have been pretty good, because we kept getting past. Until the end.

I guess we cleared a final official checkpoint, but then Vraj and Khh were stopped again. A thin, high voice hissed right near my basket.

"I recognize you two. Stop right here please. Earth sympathizers, aren't you?"

"Earth?" Vraj answered. "Some controversial little planet, isn't it? I never bother with politics. I just need to get these uniforms to the honor guards before the next ceremony. Some fool sent the wrong ones."

"There are fools here," another voice grated. "But we're not among them. Let's just take a look at these uniforms, shall we?"

My basket was jostled, and then I could feel we were running. Fast. Good thing I don't get carsick. We zigged and zagged, went up then down. Then everything got a lot darker. The uniforms were yanked off of me, and I was plucked from the basket. We were in some dark, stuffy room.

A dim light flicked on. Shasta was standing beside me. Vraj and Khh were rummaging through racks of clothing, bickering quietly.

"What happened back there?" I asked, blinking while my eyes adjusted.

"No doubt about it—those checkpoint guards were Syndicate thugs in disguise," Khh replied. "With Sorn and the others working to protect President Gifalkapul, we don't have the resources left to round up the imposters."

He turned back to the racks of clothes, pushing shirts and pants aside with his claws.

"This would do for a Torpedi disguise," Vraj said, holding up what looked like a big checked tablecloth.

"Nah, we don't have enough feet," Khh answered. "How about this outfit? They could pass as a pair of Korpawakies."

"Get real. They're way too tall for Korpawakies. Tsizzles, maybe?"

"Ridiculous," Khh snorted. "They can't even levitate."

"No, but . . . ah. The very thing! Bakabakabaka." Vraj had dragged down a big shimmery green cloak with a hood—no, two hoods.

Khh hissed in approval. He scurried over to us, pulled out something from his belt that looked like a blue magic marker, and began scribbling all over my face. Before I could flinch, he'd moved on to Shasta. Moments later I looked at her. Her face was all blue.

"Now," Vraj said, "you are a Bakabakabaka sub-assistant deputy. All we need is for this disguise to get us as far as the delegation seating area."

"Which of us is this sub-whatever?" I asked.

"You both are," Vraj snapped. With that, she grabbed us and sat each of us on one of her scaly shoulders. "Just don't wiggle. Together you weigh a ton. And keep your hands tucked in the robe. You don't have enough fingers."

Khh flew up above us and dropped the robe. For a moment we were engulfed in green cloth. Then Khh yanked until our heads fit into the two hoods. Shasta and I turned to face each other, bewildered smiles on our blue faces.

Suddenly I heard a rip behind us. Khh tore a slit in the back of the robe, crawled through, and clamped claws onto our shoulders.

"Don't yelp!" he said, after we yelped. "I'm leaving my wings outside. Bakabakabaka have 'em too. But I've got to hide the rest of me."

"You can hum, can't you?" Vraj asked from below.

"Sure," Shasta said. "But why . . ."

"Then hum. Bakabakabaka do it all the time. They don't talk much, though."

Shasta and I practiced our humming while Vraj practiced walking through the crowded aisles of the clothing room with us on her shoulders. Then we stepped out the door. A tall figure with clawed feet, two blue heads, wings, and a shimmering green robe.

"Also, don't smile," Khh hissed from his perch on our shoulders. "Bakabakabaka never smile."

Not smiling wasn't hard. Balancing on a dinosaur while a cat claws into your shoulders so that you can impersonate an alien diplomat in order to escape murderous thugs doesn't make you that jolly. I concentrated on looking serious.

I wasn't sure what to hum. "Old MacDonald Had a Farm" popped into my head, but when I started humming that Vraj jabbed my leg and snarled, "Too happy."

Shasta chimed in with "The Star-Spangled Banner," but together we were horribly off-key. Another jab. Finally we settled on "Twinkle, Twinkle Little Star."

Vraj had torn a hole in the robe so she could see out as she walked. Good thing, because this Bakabakabaka had absolutely no idea where it was going. The curved corridor we were taking was filled with aliens of all sorts and sizes. The ones I could find faces on looked like they were in serious moods. We were taller than most of the crowd, though we were dwarfed by something that looked like a cross between a giant alligator and a woolly mammoth.

I jerked with alarm and nearly fell off my perch when I saw a pair of Gnairt walking our way. From under the robe, Vraj cursed and steadied me. But she must have seen them too, because she crossed to the far side of the corridor.

The Gnairt had passed by the time we entered a larger plaza. But something worse was coming. A real Bakabakabaka.

Shasta gasped and whispered, "How do we greet a fellow . . . whatever we are?"

I had no clue. Vraj and Khh didn't give us one either. But then the other deliberately averted its gaze. Quickly I did the same, but not before noticing that a little Bakabakabaka was walking beside the big one.

"Look," it squeaked. "Uncle Kludge!"

"Shhh! Be polite," the tall one said. It gave us a fleeting glance. "Anyway, it's not your uncle. Its faces are too blue."

As the pair walked by, the little one giggled. "And anyway, this guy's got a big green tail!"

A tail? Vraj's tail must be sticking out, I thought. I hoped we'd been the only ones to hear the kid. We weren't.

The pair of Gnairt circled back. With them was a tall, celery-stalklike guy. And another nasty fairy like the first one, only blue instead of green. "Syndicate guys!" I whispered down to Vraj. "Run!"

She hitched up her robe and galloped across the plaza. Shasta and I swayed, and Khh dug in his claws even deeper. I could feel his wings behind us flapping for balance. As we barreled past a low door, it opened up and a bunch of bowling ball–shaped guys rolled out, sneering and jabbering.

Vraj tried to veer around them, but one rolled under her feet. With a screech, she catapulted through the air, landing the four of us in a writhing heap under the green robe. We clawed and scrambled our way free, but a quick look back showed our pursuers closing fast. With Vraj in the lead, we ran. I doubt she knew where we were heading anymore, just what we needed to get away from.

Dodging through the crowd, Vraj finally darted into a dimly lit hallway. We'd all just skidded around a corner when an orange fairy fluttered in front of us. Vraj growled and swatted at it, but it swerved out of reach.

"Hold off! I'm pro-Earth, like most of my people. The greens and blues are renegades. Follow me!"

Do we believe this one? Khh obviously shared my doubts. He swooped into the air, seized the fairy in a clawed fist, and hissed. "Tell the truth, or I eat you in one bite!"

"It's true," the little thing squeaked. "Our people lived there for a while once. Some of our clans had good times there, some didn't. The oranges want Earth to join. So cut the threats and follow me!"

Khh glanced at Vraj, then shrugged and let the fairy go. "All right. But remember, I'm bigger and faster than you. And probably hungrier."

The fairy nodded in midair, then swooped off to the right. We had to run full-out to follow. One hallway led to another. At the end of that one was a round doorway with silvery light past the entrance.

We all rushed up to it, then staggered to a stop. Beyond the door was nothing. Empty air dropped away below us. A long way. Desperately clutching each other, we teetered on the edge.

The orange fairy circled behind our cluster of bodies and gave us a shove.

CHAPTER TWELVE

For a moment I saw nothing but emptiness. My thought: why wasn't I an alien who can *fly*? Then there was a smooth, gold shape. I landed on it—hard. Vraj and Shasta thumped down around me. Khh flapped his wings wildly overhead.

"I've programmed this sled to go to the booth for nominated planets," a high voice said behind us. I turned to look into the eyes of the orange fairy. "The debate's already started, but you should be safe now. Supporters are guarding it."

With that, the fairy flitted back into the tunnel. The gold dish we were sitting on slowly sank down a large, airy well. The walls of the well were dotted with what looked like rooms, some enclosed, some open. All sorts of aliens were inside them, some watching screens, some peering down the well.

I peered over the edge of our sled. Way at the bottom of the well was a raised platform. Several aliens were seated on it, and one seemed to be at a podium. The scene was the same one we glimpsed on the screens in the passing rooms.

Suddenly I knew what I was looking at. The Galactic Council chamber was like a deep theater in the round, with member planets occupying rooms set into the walls like box seats. Speakers and dignitaries must be the ones on the platform below, I thought. Other gold dishes glided through the space around us as delegates went to or from their places.

Our dish halted, floating over the ledge of an empty booth. "Guess this is our stop," Vraj said as she hopped off. Shasta and I followed, and Khh swooped in overhead. We looked around.

Seats of various designs were scattered through the space, like they were meant for different species of aliens. "I wonder where this leads," Shasta said, pointing to a door at the back of our booth. I joined her just as she opened it.

Outside was a hallway. Standing around our door were a red fairy, a purple one, a large white gorilla, and a couple of guys who looked human from the waist up but then blended into the bodies of horses. Our guards?

They all smiled and nodded at us. Stunned, Shasta and I smiled and nodded back. Then we closed the door.

"Are those horse guys what I think they are?" I managed.

"Centaurs?" Shasta said. "Weird. Maybe all the creatures we think of as myths are really aliens who used to live on Earth. Or something like that."

I nodded. "This is going to take lots of re-thinking." But I quickly remembered that I had plenty of thinking to do right then.

One wall of our booth was taken up with a screen. On it was a view of what was happening on the main platform below. The guy at the podium was like one we'd seen before. Mr. Potato Head. Well, maybe not with such a goofy expression, but his head was large, brown, and lumpy, and his arms and legs were skinny sticks. Beside him were other familiar creeps: a guy looking like a scraggly black tree and two gross Gnairt.

"Doesn't look like the pro-Earth group," I muttered.

"Let's get the volume up!" Vraj said, fiddling with dials on the edge of the screen. The translation of Potato Head's speech suddenly blasted around us.

"As I have said, many of us have spent a great deal of time studying Earth's culture and history. And though it is always a joy to welcome a new species into our glorious union, we have regretfully concluded that the people of Earth are not yet ready for this honor. They are in fact woefully immature.

They are clever technologically but have not the foresight to handle technology responsibly. They have severely damaged the environment of their planet, disrupting its climate, destroying lesser species, and tolerating the impoverishment of many of their own people."

One of the Gnairt now stepped to the podium. "And what is more, these people of Earth have not only endangered their own world; they could threaten the peace of the entire galaxy! A study of their history shows them to be a hopelessly reckless, warlike people. Their technology has been devoted to developing more and more horrific weaponry. Allowing them to join our beloved Galactic Union would only loose their murderous ways upon us all!"

I scowled at their smug faces. Sure, there was a little truth in what they said, but it was all twisted and unbalanced. "That's not fair!" I yelled, shaking my fist at the screen. Of course, that helped just as much as it does when I talk back to the TV at home.

The image of a large blue mop, the Galactic President, filled the screen. But the real one or the fake?

In oily tones, he announced, "Regretfully, the delegation that was to speak on behalf of Earth's membership has chosen not to attend this assembly. In light of the evidence presented to us by these honorable speakers, I will entertain a motion to bar the planet Earth from membership in the Galactic Union and to quarantine it until such time as . . ."

He was interrupted by the sound of scuffling and angry shouts. Everyone near the podium turned in one direction. Annoyed that I couldn't see what was happening off-screen, I ran to the edge of our balcony and looked down.

On the ramp leading to the main platform, a tremendous fight had broken out. Giant centipedes grappled with each other. Some of the combatants I didn't recognize, but a few I did. Iv and Tu were wrestling with something that looked like a many-legged charcoal briquette;

Sorn was actually dueling with a walking cactus. Then onto the ramp slithered a creature with many eyes and tentacles who I'd only seen on my computer screen. Chief Galactic Patrol Agent Zythis. Behind him shuffled a second blue mop with a few of his cords singed black.

At the sight of Gifalkapul, the imposter and the earlier speakers leaped onto a hovering golden dish. But before it could zoom far, the dish was snared in a net dropped by uniformed flying slugs. Around me, I heard exclamations in so many languages that my translator implant fizzed. Creatures of all descriptions leaned out of their balconies to watch the events below.

Beside me, Shasta said, "This is better than any reality TV show."

When we looked down again, the real Galactic President stood behind the podium. "Greetings, delegates, and apologies for this indecorous scene. Regrettably, some entities had such an interest in the outcome of this debate that they felt it necessary to remove some of the participants, including myself. And I must tell you, with apologies if I sound biased, that I would not be freed from imprisonment and standing here were it not for the courage, remarkable skills, and ingenuity of our agent on Earth, as well as a native of the planet and several agents who have worked there and advocated for its admittance."

Shasta looked around our booth. "That's us, I guess. Go Earth!"

Gifalkapul continued. "But the admittance of Earth to the union is still a matter for our membership to decide. You have read the material; you have heard arguments in opposition. Now you can hear from supporters, who incidentally only failed to attend earlier because they were likewise forcibly detained."

He now looked directly up at our booth. "I would like to first call upon Earth native Shasta O'Neil and the planted agent and Galactic Union envoy Zackary Gaither."

I suddenly felt shriveled inside. Me? Down there? Speaking in front of all these very, very alien aliens? All of them watching me with whatever they had for eyes? Me on all of their screens?

Beside me Shasta said, "Right. Let's go."

It took her and the others to shove me onto the golden dish hovering nearby. Then the two of us glided down to the platform. We shook hands or tentacles or whatever all around, and then I was standing at the podium. I closed my eyes and tried to pretend I was standing in front of class, giving a report. That used to scare me enough. Now it seemed like nothing.

"Hello. I'm Zack Gaither. I was born on Izbor, but I grew up as a human on Earth. It's a great place. Sure, some of what those other guys said was kind of true. Humans have fought wars and have sort of messed up their environment. But they also can make peace. They can learn from mistakes and are trying to fix the environment. And they have great art and music. They're always trying to make new stuff and learn new things."

Feeling a little more comfortable now, I glanced at Tu and Iv and suddenly remembered how we'd met at Roswell at a UFO festival. "One of the things they've always wanted to learn about," I continued, "is you people. They're always hoping that they're not alone in the universe. They invent ways to study the universe, and when they don't have proof that you're out here, they make up stories about you, hoping someday to find that the stories are true. So, please, don't disappoint them. Let them know that you're as wise and understanding and exciting as they hope you are. Let them join you."

I'd kind of run out of words. But there was more that needed saying. "But like I said, I'm not actually an Earth human. Listen to somebody who is." I looked at Shasta and felt myself blushing. "She's a really remarkable person. I hope you all give yourself a chance to meet people like her. I'm glad I did."

Shasta looked at me. Was she blushing too? Clearing her throat, she stepped to the podium. "Zack has said things very well. Yes, Earth people have made mistakes. But haven't you, all of you? I don't know your histories, but I can't believe you haven't all had bad times and done things you regretted. But you kept trying to do better, kept working for what you knew was right. And finally you got here. And as an Earth human, I'm really glad to be here with you now. Like Zack said, we've been dreaming about it for a long time."

She looked at me and then continued. "So it's up to you. You can make those dreams come true. Yes, Earth could use some help, but you can give that help. My grandfather was a very wise man. One thing he taught me was that we must help one another, that we can learn from one another. Another thing was that we are all part of everything. Of rocks, of trees, of oceans, and all life. And of the stars. Please help us to finally be part of those stars."

When she stepped back, I squeezed her hand and whispered, "You were great."

"I was scared. *You* were great." Then she grinned. "I guess we make a good team."

I liked that thought. I'd never been much at team sports. But here, I guess, the goal was worth it. Of course, people are always saying it's how you play the game that counts, not winning or losing. And win or lose, this game had been fun to play—if you don't count all the pain, terror, and times we'd nearly gotten killed.

Still, I really wanted to win this one.

CHAPTER THIRTEEN

After we had spoken, others did as well. Sorn, Vraj, Khh, Iv, and Tu all talked about what they had learned about Earth and why we should be allowed to join the union. Even Chief Agent Zythis spoke on our behalf. I had to concentrate on listening to him instead of just watching all his eye flaps and tentacles waving about.

We returned to our booth and waited nervously for the voting to get under way. A big tally sheet was shown on the screen. Shasta and I stared at it, but we couldn't read the writing. It looked like a chicken had stepped in green ink and trotted over the page. Sorn fiddled with some buttons at the side of the screen. The chicken scratches dissolved and were replaced by the standard English alphabet. Not that it helped much. The list of member planets was incredibly long, and most of them had names that seemed impossible to pronounce in any language.

Red lights began to pop up on the screen in the "yes" and "no" columns. Sorn told us that each delegation had to vote within itself before casting the final vote for its planet. I could hear arguments echoing around the huge, deep gallery. It seemed that maybe our pro-Earth speeches had persuaded some folks, and so had the fact that the bad guys had tried to swing the vote by kidnapping the Galactic President. But it also sounded like the Kiapa Kapa arguments had convinced some aliens to vote against us.

The red dots kept mounting in both columns. It looked nearly even to me. My insides twisted into knots. Then I noticed that one block of votes hadn't come in yet.

"What's with those planets?" I asked Sorn as she looked intensely at the screen.

"That's the Huuwii Confederacy. An alliance of mostly water worlds. They can be ornery and pretty negative about change. I only hope they'll like the fact that Earth has a lot of oceans."

I glanced out our balcony, looking over at the cluster of Huuwii delegates. Their booths looked like giant fishbowls—gilled, grey-green water people gestured back and forth inside water-filled glass domes. Suddenly, Khh and Vraj began squealing and shouting behind me.

I spun around. A clump of red dots had appeared in the "yes" column. Earth had won! It would be invited to join the union!

I hugged Shasta. We hugged everybody. We flung open the doors and hugged all the guards outside. We taught several species how to do high fives.

More business, of course, came up before the Galactic Council, but I was too excited and overwhelmed to pay much attention. What did catch my attention was what happened after the meeting adjourned. We partied!

Sorn arranged for a big room, music, lots of food and drink, and a whole lot of guests. Those guests included fairies (red, purple, and yellow), horse-men, Vraj's dinosaur relatives, and a bunch of delegates who must have voted with us. They ranged from quivering jelly blobs (strawberry) to ten-foot-high walking pinecones, floating wind chimes, and something like a cross between a pin-cushion and a four-headed giraffe. Chief Agent Zythis and President Gifalkapul even dropped in for a while. You should see the president dance! Oh yeah, and there was that large white gorilla from the council chamber who I think is distantly related to Bigfoot.

It was some party. Some of the food and music were even recognizable as food and music. Everybody seemed eager to celebrate the admittance of an obscure little planet called Earth. I really had a great time, but I have to admit that I fell asleep partway through and woke up much later, snuggled into bed in our guest rooms.

Then there were more serious days, planning how to formally contact Earth, let humans know about the Galactic Union, and arrange for them to join it. That's when I started feeling nervous again. I would have a big role in all of that. And despite all I'd gone through, I had to admit I was still basically a kid.

"Don't worry," Sorn said one time when I was doing exactly that. "You've proven you can handle much tougher assignments, and this is what you've been training for all your life, before you even knew it."

"Yes, but having to talk to presidents and kings and prime ministers and address millions of people on television? Me, Zack Gaither. I'm not even in high school yet!"

"Hey," Shasta said, "you helped free the president of the entire galaxy, and you talked in front of hundreds of majorly weird aliens. This will be a piece of cake."

"And you'll hardly be alone," Sorn added.

"There'll be a whole delegation from the Galactic Union and . . ."

"And me," Shasta put in. "I'm not getting left out now. After all, my grandfather told me my destiny was with the star spirits."

With all these pep talks, I was feeling a little better by the time we headed back to Earth. The ship was much bigger and fancier than the one we'd left on. It was fun to explore and have the crew explain stuff to me like I wasn't just a kid.

But when the viewscreen finally showed Earth below us, all blue and white and beautiful, I felt small and big all at the same time.

That was home down there, no matter where I'd been born. They didn't know it yet, but all the people living there were about to have their lives changed forever. And so was I.

Sorn told me it would be months, maybe a year yet, before I had to take on my envoy duties. Apparently a lot of preparations still needed to be made. So, for a while longer, I could go to school and be an almost normal kid. My parents already knew, of course, and I'd have to explain some things to Ken.

Then a terrific thought hit me and pushed some of the worry away. Maybe I could stretch my normal life out through next October. After all I'd seen, I had some truly awesome ideas for Halloween costumes.

COMING SOON

From the mind of Pamela F. Service,
author of the Alien Agent series,
comes a new adventure:

WRITE OUT OF
THIS WORLD

JOSHUA loves to write

wild sci-fi stories. He dreams

of being a famous author.

But he's about to discover

that the stories he

thought he'd imagined are

REAL.

RECEIVING TRANSMISSION FROM

WRITE OUT OF
THIS WORLD

BOOK ONE

DOWNLOADING....

"Shhh!" I put my argument with Maggie on hold. The sudden movement in the woods had snatched my attention. "The blue guys."

Maggie rolled her eyes. She's really good at that. "You think I'll fall for that? Beware the big bad Cub Scouts."

I didn't know what the creatures coming from the woods were, but they were not Cub Scouts. Grabbing Maggie's hand, I dragged her out of the clearing. She squawked, looked behind us, and turned silent. I didn't have to drag her any more.

We crashed through the edge of the woods, bursting into the open and running across the bare construction site. I guess *running* isn't the word since we began to slip and slide in the red mud. I glanced behind. The blue guys weren't having much trouble. They were gaining. Before we passed the yellow bulldozer, they had us surrounded.

For the first time I got a good look at them. I wished I hadn't.

They were tall, flat, and faceless, sort of like big sticks of gum—blue gum. The tops of their heads were fluttering strips. Other strips flapped at the ends of their noodly arms and legs. The creatures were so skinny that when they turned sideways, they almost disappeared. I could hardly read their expressions, but nothing about them seemed friendly.

One of the blue guys wiggled the strips at the top of its head. A thin, grating sound filled the air. Was that talking? Two others leapt forward and stuffed what looked like hairnets on top of my and Maggie's heads. I struggled to yank mine off until I noticed that the blue guys' odd sounds had become chirpy English. *The nets must be translator things*, I realized. I stopped tugging.

"Good," one of them chirped. "Intelligent enough not to fight. You. Taller one. You are the Joshua P. Higgins. Correct?"

For a moment, I just stared, trying to force sound out past the fear in my throat. "Yes," I finally managed.

"Author of *Danger on Yastol*?"

"What? You mean . . . Well, sure, I wrote it." I felt like giggling wildly. What were these guys, book critics? Fans?

"Good. You will take us there."

"Where?"

This thing is getting majorly weird, I thought.

"You want to go to the bookstore? Buy a copy?"

"Have copies. You take us to Yastol."

I laughed. "You've got to be kidding. That's not a real place. I just made it up."

The creature grunted. "Not intelligent after all. You humans are actualizers. You can tune in to other worlds. One of the few species in the universe. You write about them in what you call *fiction*."

"Wait a minute!" Maggie interrupted, disbelief on her face. "You mean all these books and stories people write, . . . they're just describing the way things are someplace else?"

"Correct. What are you, shorter person? Does Joshua P. Higgins need you for his work?"

"What? Oh sure. I'm his critic. He can't write anything without me telling him where it stinks."

"I do not understand. But will accept. You come too. . . ."

<END TRANSMISSION>

about the author

Pamela F. Service has written more than twenty books in the science fiction, fantasy, and nonfiction genres. After working as a history museum curator for many years in Indiana, she became the director of a museum in Eureka, California, where she lives with her husband and cats. She is also active in community theater, politics, and beachcombing.